& Revenge

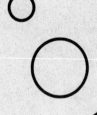

...*Plus!*

IS SHE **REALLY** YOUR BEST MATE?
TRY OUR FAB QUIZ AT
THE BACK OF THE BOOK

SOME SECRETS ARE JUST TOO GOOD TO KEEP TO YOURSELF!

Sugar
SECRETS...

...& Revenge

Mel Sparke

Collins

An Imprint of HarperCollinsPublishers

Published in Great Britain by Collins in 1999
Collins is an imprint of HarperCollins Publishers Ltd
77–85 Fulham Palace Road, Hammersmith, London W6 8JB

The HarperCollins website address is
www.fireandwater.com

9 8 7 6 5 4 3 2

ISBN 0 00 675439 2

Printed and bound in Great Britain by
Caledonian International Book Manufacturing Ltd, Glasgow

With thanks to Marina Gask

CHAPTER 1

• •

MATT THE LOVE-RAT

"And Matt's *always* telling me how gorgeous I am, which is sweet of him. And he's *sooo* attentive! He's really into me, you know..."

Catrina Osgood took a break from bragging and squinted into the mirror to apply a third coat of black mascara. She grinned triumphantly at her reflected view of Sonja and Kerry. The two girls smiled back, barely stifling their yawns and, as Catrina looked away to start work on the other set of spidery lashes, they grimaced at each other. They'd heard it all before. Plenty of times. The only difference being that instead of boasting about some conquest from school or college, or wherever else Cat got her claws into a lad, this time she was talking about one of their own crowd.

Flicking her silky blonde mane over one shoulder and nonchalantly inspecting her nails, Sonja Harvey snorted scornfully.

"Yeah, but remember what he's like, Cat. Before you two started going out together, Matt was also 'into' half the girls in sixth form, so I don't know why you're getting so excited."

Sonja winked at Kerry Bellamy, who giggled and adjusted her wire-rimmed specs, something she often did when she couldn't think of anything else to say. To be honest, none of the friends in their crowd knew what to make of Matt and Catrina's romance. In the few weeks it had been going on, the two of them had spent most of their time snogging each other silly, which made uncomfortable viewing for Sonja, Kerry, Maya and Ollie – never mind making shy-boy Joe positively squirm.

Blusher brush in hand, Catrina slowly shook her head at her cousin's reflection. "Well, Sonja, that's just 'cause he hasn't gone out with anyone like *me* before. And let's face it, now that he has, he won't be looking around for something better..."

Kerry, sick of watching Catrina preening and equally fed up with finding fault with her own reflection, gazed at her feet instead. Her new pink wedge shoes were pinching like crazy, but at least she'd painted her toenails this time. Then Kerry groaned inwardly as she noticed that the cherry red varnish on one big toenail was already chipped. Darn! How had that happened?

She glanced over at Sonja's toes, immaculate and freshly painted in gleaming silver. *Perfect as ever*, mused Kerry woefully. But then, with her honey-blonde hair, bright blue eyes and enviably athletic figure, Sonja always did look perfect. It was a fact of life.

"No, of *course* not, Cat," said Sonja, her voice dripping with sarcasm. "I mean, why would he stray now that he's going out with every lad's dream girl?"

"Oh, yes – you can mock all you like, Miss Sonja Smug-face, but I know this is special." Catrina had moved on to her lips, which she was coating thickly with Very Berry lipstick, pouting in an exaggerated manner into the mirror. Her dyed blonde hair was piled on top of her head in a messy knot, with bits falling sexily around her face. Not, Kerry noted cheerfully, that this hid the fact that her dark roots were showing.

As Cat turned round to face them and adjusted her clingy velvet top, the two girls got an eyeful of her ample cleavage. One thing Catrina had never been was subtle. In more ways than one.

"It's so nice having a boyfriend as lovely as

Matt. I really would recommend it to anyone who's never tried it..."

Kerry pushed her glasses back on her nose and blushed furiously, knowing this comment was aimed particularly at her.

"No thanks, Cat, he's more your type – shallow and short-term," snapped Sonja.

She liked Matt, but was under no illusions about how he behaved when it came to girls. And her cousin Catrina could be great fun, but she had a real knack of getting on people's nerves, just like now. And it wasn't as if the girls had come to Ollie Stanton's seventeenth birthday party to be wound up by Catrina – they had better things to do.

Before Cat could snap back, Sonja nudged Kerry to let her know the conversation was over and started heading for the door, pushing past the queue of staring, silent girls who'd been enjoying the free show while they waited their turn for the loos.

"What *is* she like?" groaned Sonja, the second they were out and on their way back to the function room of Ollie's parents' pub, The Swan. "Why does she always have to be so competitive when it comes to boys? Like we *care* or something."

"I know," nodded Kerry. "I mean, she's a laugh and everything—"

The two girls looked at each other and broke into ironic smiles.

"Well, *most* of the time," Kerry grinned. "But when she starts all that bragging, it's so annoying. And *very* boring."

Sonja grinned back and then, with a flick of her shiny hair, she headed off towards the dance floor, yelling "I love this one!" at Kerry, who hurried to keep up with her.

Weaving through the tables, Sonja clocked how many people were dancing already – which just went to show what a brilliant DJ Matt Ryan was; he always managed to pick the right tracks to get everyone going. But before she could join the other dancers, Sonja's path was suddenly blocked by another friend, Maya Joshi, whose eyes were wide with alarm. This was weird. Maya never looked worried about anything. Ever.

"Sonny, it's Matt – he's getting off with someone!" she yelled above the music. Sonja glanced in the direction Maya was pointing and gasped. Catching her up, Kerry followed Sonja's gaze – and froze. Sure enough, there was Matt behind his desk – the same Matt that Catrina had just been bragging about – wrapped around a slim brunette. In full view of the entire dance floor.

Sonja made a snap decision. She was going to have to run back and stop Cat from walking in on this. Sick of Cat's showing-off she might have been, but Sonja knew Catrina didn't deserve this kind of humiliation.

And however much she might have felt like saying "I told you so", Sonja wasn't about to rub her cousin's nose in it. No, it would be far better for Cat to hear what was happening from someone on *her* side, rather than finding out the hard – and very public – way. Otherwise, the fur would fly. Otherwise, Ollie's night would very probably be ruined.

"Wait here," she mouthed at Kerry and Maya, before heading back towards the loos.

But it was too late. Swinging her hips and jangling her many bracelets to the funky track, Catrina was heading their way, dancing and grinning like the cat who'd got the cream, through the swarms of friends and family that had turned up for Ollie and his twin sister Natasha's birthday bash.

Automatically, Sonja, Kerry and Maya turned as one and peered over towards the DJ desk.

After all, the kiss – and the danger – could be over.

But it wasn't.

• • •

When Sonja and Kerry had left her, Catrina didn't hurry to give up her place at the mirror. It suited her just fine to spend a few more moments on her appearance before returning to the party.

Squirting a last-minute spritz of Issey Miyake on her wrists (and just a dab down the front of her velvet top), Catrina felt like Queen of the Night. She was in a brilliant mood. She knew she looked good, she knew most of the teenage female population of Winstead were jealous of the boyfriend she'd landed, *and* she'd just rubbed her snooty cousin Sonja's nose in it. All that stuff about her and Kerry not being bothered about having boyfriends – who were they kidding?

Cat smoothed her top straight yet again and smiled a smug smile of contentment. At sixteen years of age, she was still a devotee of the old-style Ginger Spice school of self-expression. She knew what her limitations were – being OK-looking rather than supermodel gorgeous – but she was fearless when it came to knock-'em-dead outfits and movie star make-up.

She loved attracting attention and invariably she got it; in fact, she'd lost count of the number of boys she'd been out with. If she was honest with herself, she'd never really felt anything for any of them, but she adored being centre-stage in other people's lives.

But with Matt it was different. He was something special. She'd fallen for him the minute Ollie had introduced him to the crowd, which had been some time last summer, when he'd finished at his posh boarding school and moved back home with his dad full time.

Sure, he loved himself a bit too much, but in Cat's opinion, anyone that good-looking, with his own car and whose father was a rich property developer, was completely justified in fancying himself. It had just frustrated her how long it had taken him to fancy her back.

Matt had finally got the message three weeks ago when they'd all been hanging out at his house one Saturday night, watching a horror video with the lights out for dramatic effect. Catrina had managed to snuggle up beside Matt on the beanbags, and kept grabbing him in the scary moments.

All that enforced hugging seemed to have done the trick. By the time the credits rolled and Ollie had jumped up to put the lights on, the two friends were very much in snog mode – much to everyone's surprise. And that was it; Matt and Catrina were officially an item and Cat was utterly smitten.

"Cat! Er... can you help me?" The sound of Sonja's voice jolted Catrina out of her reverie.

"I–I've got something in my eye," Sonja blinked, grabbing hold of Cat's elbow and steering her backwards. "Can you come to the loo with me for a minute?"

Oh, for God's sake! thought Catrina. *Do I have to?*

She'd left Matt nearly half an hour ago and was now impatient to get back to him. He'd think she'd got lost at this rate. Catrina impatiently wriggled free of Sonja's grasp and reached into her tiny beaded handbag, pulling out her lighter. Holding the flame up to Sonja's face, she squinted as she tried to peer into her cousin's eye.

"Sorry, Son, can't see a thing," she shrugged, flicking her lighter shut. "Must run, I've got far more important things to do..."

Pushing past Sonja, Cat was momentarily perplexed to find mousy Miss Kerry barring her way. She appeared to be trying to speak but Cat wasn't in the mood to listen.

"Move it, Kerry!" she said in her usual tactless way, side-stepping her friend. "Matt'll be wondering where I—"

The crowds in front of her seemed to part at that split second and Catrina was instantly struck dumb. There was Matt – her Matt – entangled with some girl... some girl who looked strangely familiar.

As if suddenly aware that they had an audience, Matt and the girl stopped snogging and pulled apart. Matt seemed to be scanning the room frantically... then his eyes locked on to Catrina's ferocious stare.

With no new track lined up to take its place – the DJ having been otherwise distracted – the music faded to nothing, leaving a silent room as everyone held their breath.

CHAPTER 2

● ●

CAT LASHES OUT

"Get your filthy hands off him!" shrieked Catrina, practically bursting the eardrums of most of the party guests. "He's *mine!*"

The slim, brown-haired girl turned to face the snarling Cat, who suddenly recognised her as Ollie's twin sister, Natasha. As Cat stormed towards them, Natasha flashed a confused look at Matt, then retreated fast.

Half howling, half screeching, Cat lunged at a pint glass of beer on the table nearest her – and chucked the contents of it smack into Matt's stunned face.

"Watch out for my decks!" he yelled, pointing down at his precious sound system.

"Your decks?! Who cares about your *decks*?" Cat screamed back. "What the *hell* were you doing with *her*?"

His hair drenched and his face shiny with the dripping beer, Matt held up his hands in a gesture of innocence. "Woah, Cat! Calm down! It was only Tasha!"

"Yes, I could see that for myself, thank you very much!" Cat bit back, her eyes blazing.

"I was just giving her a birthday kiss!"

"And you needed to use your *tongue* for that, did you?" she spat.

"Oh come on, Cat..." Matt half laughed, licking his lips as the beer trickled down his face.

Watching in stunned silence, Sonja, Kerry and Maya all cringed inwardly – laughing at Cat wasn't a very good idea in the circumstances.

"What d'you mean, 'Come on, Cat'?" she mimicked, before taking an almighty swing at him. Matt ducked just in time to avoid being punched in the face.

This only made Cat all the more furious. "You're a waste of space, Matthew Ryan! You're *scum!* You're a two-timing bas—"

Matt dodged another flying punch. With no target for her fist to connect with, Cat lost her balance and tumbled sideways, bringing down the nearest table and its contents with her. At that point, Matt lost it – helplessly laughing out loud as he reached down and offered her a hand up.

Infuriated with him and mortified at finding herself in such an undignified position, Catrina landed a couple of stinging slaps on Matt's arms.

"Ow! Ouch! Cat, you're over-reacting! It was just a friendly kiss! It didn't mean anything..." protested Matt, trying to sound apologetic, but still finding it hard to stop laughing.

Just as Cat tried to spring at him from the floor, claws at the ready, a pair of strong hands gripped her by the wrists and pulled her upright.

"Now, Catrina, let's just calm down, shall we?" said Ollie's dad placatingly. "I don't want any nonsense in my pub tonight. We're all supposed to be enjoying ourselves."

Her rage suddenly stilled, Cat felt waves of embarrassment wash over her. Quickly, she glanced around the room and saw countless eyes upon her.

She saw her three girlfriends; she saw Ollie and Joe standing in the doorway carrying musical equipment and obviously wondering what the hell was going on; and she saw Ollie's mum and that bitch of a sister. Her gaze returned to Ollie's dad, Stuart, who was still holding on to her firmly and looking at her as if she were some sort of mad woman.

"It's not my fault!" she whimpered, suddenly realising that she was being portrayed as the unreasonable one in all this. "It's him!"

From his position of safety, Matt peered over Stuart Stanton's shoulder and gave her a cheeky grin and a wink.

Maya rushed over and put her arms round Cat just as she burst into tears of hurt and anger.

• • •

"This is a party, remember, so let's all get back to having a good time!" said Stuart Stanton into the mike as Matt hurriedly got the music up and running again.

"What was all that about?" asked Ollie, dumping the amp he'd been carrying on the floor, and looking from his father to his friend Matt.

"I'll let Matthew explain," said his dad dryly. "I think I'd better go and see how your sister's doing."

"Matt?" Ollie said questioningly, wondering why Matt's dark hair and T-shirt were soaking. Along with Joe and the other boys in his band, The Loud, he'd been outside getting their gear together for the set they were about to play and had only caught the tail-end of the drama.

"Oh, this is good, Ollie," Sonja butted in, staring angrily at Matt. "*He* only went and snogged your sister in front of everyone."

"Natasha?" Ollie exclaimed. "What are you playing at, Matt?"

Matt grinned sheepishly and shrugged. "Well, she *is* gorgeous, Ollie..."

Sonja, Kerry and Joe stood open-mouthed at his cheek.

"And that's your excuse, is it?" said Ollie, tight-lipped. "Christ, no wonder Cat went ballistic!" He turned to the girls, concern written all over his face. "Do you think she's OK?" Ollie could never stand to see people unhappy – especially one of his own friends.

"Don't worry, Ollie – Maya's calming her down. She's good at that," said Kerry reassuringly.

"Come on, Kerry, let's go and lend some moral support," suggested Sonja, shooting another withering glance at Matt. Linking arms with her friend, they headed off to the Ladies.

"Well done, mate!" said Ollie, now the three boys were alone. Both Joe and Matt looked confused.

"What do you mean?" asked Matt, looking at his friend's serious expression.

"This little event wasn't exactly good for the party vibe, you know what I mean? And apart from killing the atmosphere stone-dead, you've ruined my sister's birthday *and* treated your girlfriend like dirt. That's quite an achievement!"

"But– but, Ollie," Matt tried to protest, shrugging again and grinning a lads-together grin, "it was just a bit of a flirt! Just a bit of fun!"

"Didn't look like anybody was laughing much," chipped in Joe.

"Except you," added Ollie, his face like thunder.

Matt dropped the smile. It had finally hit him just how less than impressed his whole crowd were.

• • •

Perched on the edge of a sink, Catrina was weeping and hiccuping so much she was almost incoherent.

"I'll–I'll m-m-make him sorry... No one does that to me... And *her*, she– she's – hic! – nothing c-c-compared to me..."

"It's not Natasha's fault," said Maya, trying to be fair to Ollie's sister. "She probably didn't even know you two were an item."

"Yeah, why would she?" Sonja agreed. "She hasn't been back in Winstead for months and Ollie said she only flew in from Milan yesterday 'specially for the party, remember?"

"She– she's still a b-b-bitch," sniffed Cat. She wasn't exactly in the mood to forgive. Especially

22

not someone as beautiful and sensational as Natasha Stanton.

At only just seventeen, Ollie's sister had been a successful model for over a year. She lived in a flash flat in central London with other drop-dead gorgeous models, and had a jet-setting lifestyle that her old schoolmates could only dream of.

"Matt's the one to blame," Maya reiterated, "so don't waste your time being angry with Natasha."

Cat nodded numbly.

"And don't waste your time being angry with him either – he's not worth it," said Sonja, handing Cat another piece of loo roll to blow her nose on. "In fact, why don't you just go back out there and show him what a great time you can have without him? We'll all be with you!"

It was the sort of fighting talk that usually got Cat going, but it didn't seem to be working tonight.

"I can't go out there! All those p-p-people saw..." she trailed off, sobbing again.

That's it: we're obviously fated to spend our evening in this loo, thought Kerry grimly, aware of the sound of The Loud launching into their first number in the function room.

She caught Sonja's eye and discreetly tapped her watch. It was one thing that Catrina's night had been ruined, but they couldn't let Ollie down on his birthday – he'd want to know all his friends were there to witness the first ever performance of his and Joe's band.

"Cat – that's the band on. Everyone will be watching them, not you," said Sonja, smiling encouragingly and gently pushing her cousin's hair back off her damp face. "And we should be out there too – Ollie and Joe will want our support."

Catrina looked up and nodded meekly, then started groping around inside her bag for a cigarette. Normally, they all moaned at her for smoking, but this time the girls let it pass.

"OK, let's do it," she said defiantly, before turning round and spotting her reflection in the mirror, catching sight of her puffy, mascara-stained face. "God, look what he's done to me!"

The others groaned silently, knowing it would take a serious make-up session before Cat would be ready to face the world.

● ● ●

The Swan's function room wasn't huge, but it was packed and Ollie felt a massive buzz as he gave it all he'd got from the tiny stage. Behind him, Mick the guitarist, Rob the bass player and

Joe on drums sounded as if they were holding it all together.

They'd decided not to inflict much of their own stuff on the audience tonight, but to do a whole load of cover versions: newer tracks their friends would be into, plus some old '70s rock songs (Ollie had promised his Uncle Nick) and a few Motown classics (his mum and dad's favourite – and the sort of stuff he and Natasha had been brought up on).

This beats the day job, he laughed to himself, thinking of the End-of-the-Line café and the position he held there as cook-cum-waiter-cum-dogsbody.

At the front of the stage, a group of girls started giggling and screaming at him. *And you don't get many girls screaming at you for serving them doughnuts and milkshakes either...*

It was just as he was launching into his 'Thank you and goodnight' speech at the end of the set that Ollie caught sight of a puffy-eyed Cat elbowing her way through the party-goers and heading purposefully towards the stage.

"Uh-oh, here comes trouble," he turned and mouthed at Joe, who looked as if he'd just spotted a ten-ton truck approaching. Ollie turned back to face the audience just as Cat stepped up on to the stage and grabbed the mike from his hand.

She pointed a scarlet-nailed finger in the direction of the DJ desk and, in a voice that would have worked well in the horror movie that had first brought them together, Cat let out a menacing growl.

"*You* will *pay*, Matthew Ryan."

CHAPTER 3

• •

MATT MAKES IT WORSE

Late next morning, Kerry Bellamy was still in her bed. She was watching her portable TV with Lewis, her six-year-old brother, perched on the end of the bed and Barney, their slobbery dog, curled up on the floor next to them.

There was something reassuring about cartoons and Kerry found it comforting to go through this weekend routine, just the three of them. But she was going to be late if she didn't get a move on.

The End-of-the-Line café was always packed on Saturday mornings and Kerry knew that if you didn't get there early, there was almost no chance of getting a table. And the crowd would definitely need one today.

"You'll take root in that bed if you don't get up

soon, young lady!" Kerry heard her mum yell up the stairs.

She knew her mum hated her 'moping around in her room', as she called it, and was always on at Kerry to get up and do something useful.

For once, Kerry wasn't going to argue. She had arranged to meet Sonja, Maya and Catrina at 11.30 in the End. They had some serious sorting out to do. The events of the previous night needed to be discussed, Cat would need further consoling and the girls would have to decide how best to handle this messy turn of events – the future of the crowd depended on it. It would be awful if this Matt and Catrina crisis split them all up.

It probably wasn't the kind of 'useful' Kerry's mum had in mind, but she'd have to lump it.

"OK! OK! I'm not deaf y'know!" Kerry called down, already up and on her way to the bathroom.

After a quick shower and brush of her teeth, Kerry spent her usual ten minutes checking despairingly in the mirror to see if she'd miraculously become beautiful overnight.

"Still no joy, then," she tutted, pulling her unruly reddish-brown curls around and trying out different poses and facial expressions. She jumped when she realised Lewis was lurking outside, peeking at her through the crack in the door. "C'mon, Lew, give me some peace, will you!"

He disappeared from view and she heard him thundering downstairs yelling "PEACEPEACEPEACE! Kerry wants a piece of CAKE!" at the top of his lungs.

"Not that I'm likely to get any peace round here," she muttered to her reflection, before heading back to her room to get dressed.

Putting her watch on, she noticed it was 11.15 already. No time for preening – it'd just have to be jeans and her blue fleece again.

Oh well, she thought, *looks like I'm not going to break any hearts today – but then, why change the habit of a lifetime?*

● ● ●

Miraculously, the girls had managed to nab their favourite table, right in the bay window of the café.

"Hi, Kez," said Sonja, grinning at her friend as she walked in the door.

Kerry smiled a hello at Maya and Sonja, then turned her gaze to Cat to gauge how her mood was today. Not good by the looks of it.

"Er, feeling better?" she asked uselessly.

"No," Cat responded sharply, her eyes still red-rimmed from a night's-worth of tears. "That pig..."

"Er, well, I'm just going to get a coffee. Do you want anything?" Kerry was keen to help, but she always felt a bit inadequate around Catrina – even when she was at a low ebb like this – and trusted that Sonja and Maya were going to do the bulk of the emotional sorting out.

"OK," nodded Cat. "Hot chocolate and marshmallow, please. With extra marshmallow. And a chocolate croissant, if they've got any left."

Sonja rolled her eyes to the ceiling. Trust Cat not to let grief get in the way of her appetite.

Weaving through the packed tables, Kerry made her way over to the counter to order.

"Hello?" she said, peering over the metal-topped surface and through into the kitchen. "Is anyone there?"

She nearly jumped out of her skin when Ollie's face popped up only inches in front of hers.

"Oh, hi, Kerry! Sorry – didn't mean to make you jump. I was just—" he dropped his voice to a whisper, "starting to dig my escape tunnel down there!"

Kerry looked at the spoon he was brandishing.

"I think you'd get on faster with a spade," she joked back. "And let's face it, your Uncle Nick's never going to let you go that easily!"

Ollie had agreed to help out temporarily in his uncle's café – the End-of-the-Line – when he'd quit school the year before, but had never quite managed to find anything better.

"Tell me about it!" grinned Ollie.

He had the best grin in the world. It made his whole face light up and he looked like a big kid who'd just heard the funniest joke ever. In fact, Kerry realised, Ollie always looked like an overgrown kid, with his huge hazel eyes, mop top of floppy brown hair and permanently amused expression.

Leaning one elbow on the counter and cupping his chin in his hand, he asked, "So what'll it be then, Kez?"

"A coffee and a hot chocolate with double marshmallow, please, Ol. Oh, and a chocolate croissant."

"Wow, you're going wild today," he teased, reaching over for the serving tongs.

"It's not for me, it's for Cat," she smiled, nodding over in the direction of the bay window booth. "We're on a mission to take her mind off... well, y'know."

"Don't I!" nodded Ollie, pulling out a tray and beginning to load her order on board. "I nipped over when it was quiet earlier and got the whole story again from Cat."

"How's Natasha? It didn't spoil her birthday too much, did it?" Kerry asked.

She didn't know Natasha very well – none of the crowd did apart from Ollie. Natasha'd had her own little posse at school and, since she'd been talent-spotted, had always been away during weekends and holidays. They'd seen even less of her in the last year since she'd taken up modelling full time.

"She was a bit shaken up, but she's all right," Ollie shrugged. "She had no idea that Matt was going out with someone, of course. He can be such a sly one..."

Ollie and Matt had become mates after Matt had found himself at a serious loose end and friendless after his years-long stint at boarding school. As a budding (but as yet not very successful) DJ, he'd drifted into a nodding acquaintance with Ollie's uncle, Nick, when he'd discovered the second-hand record shop that Nick ran. As often as not, he'd end up in the café next door that Nick also owned.

Nick, a former roadie and 'big mate' of practically every band ever known (according to him), loved having an audience to tell his long-winded muso tales to, and Matt was more than happy to listen.

Ollie, who'd grown up with his uncle's musical

sagas, still got a kick out of listening to them too, even though he took most of them with a very big pinch of salt. Once Ollie got to know Matt, it was only a matter of time before the rest of the crowd got to know him too, even though he was a year or so older than most of them.

He was friendly and easy-going – the fact that he had a huge house, his own den and a car to ferry everyone around in didn't hurt either – and so he fitted in well with everyone. Until now.

"Well, I know he's been sly with a few girls since he landed in Winstead, but I wish he hadn't done it to one of us," sighed Kerry. "I mean, who knows what Cat'll do, after that little speech on stage last night?"

"You know what they say about 'Hell hath no fury like a Cat scorned'," said Ollie wryly. "Still, I reckon he'll talk her round. Don't you, Kez?"

"What, after she chucked a drink over him and threatened him in public? I doubt it, Ol. Mind you, she was so smitten by him, you never know..."

By the time Kerry got the tray back to the table, Maya was dishing out some of her infinite wisdom.

"Stop thinking about ways to 'get' him, Cat. Just try to ignore him and get on with having a good time. It'll probably infuriate him much more when he realises that you're not heartbroken. That's the best revenge." Maya tucked her long, dark hair behind one ear and picked a stray flake of chocolate from Catrina's croissant.

Cat looked thoughtful – Maya always managed to get through to people.

"Yeah, I guess you're right."

"It's true, isn't it, Sonny?" said Maya, keen for back-up now that Cat seemed to be in the mood to see sense.

But Sonja wasn't listening. She'd just spotted a disturbing sight outside in the street. And half a second later, Catrina spotted it too.

Matt was strolling along the opposite pavement, hand in hand with Natasha.

CHAPTER 4

● ●

OLLIE TO THE RESCUE

"The nerve of him! The complete and utter nerve! Just look at him, the slimy little toad!" shrieked Catrina, jumping to her feet.

The other girls round the table all gasped in unison. Was Matt being insensitive or just stupid? Did he seriously *want* another fight like the night before? And what had got into Natasha's head after everything that had happened?

Catrina's eyes might have been flashing dangerously but, Sonja noted, her bottom lip had begun to tremble. It really was too much!

"Ollie! Ollie – have you seen this?" Sonja bellowed over the café. "Sort it out will you? I think it's time you had a word with your dodgy mate *and* your sister."

Ollie came out from behind the counter to see

what they were all looking at... and groaned. Matt *really* was out of order this time.

"Yep, OK, in a sec, Son..."

That morning, as well as his usual workload, Ollie'd been lumbered with settling the new girl, Anna Michaels, into her job at the café and didn't want to leave her on her own for too long. He poked his head into the kitchen where he'd left her peeling potatoes.

"I, erm, have to do something for a minute. Will you be OK?"

Luckily, Anna seemed the capable sort.

"Sure – I'll be fine. Do what you've got to do," she smiled easily and followed him through to the counter.

Giving her a quick thumbs-up sign, Ollie zigzagged through the tables, hauled open the door and shouted after Matt and Natasha.

"C'mon, Matt," said Ollie breathlessly, having run across the road to catch up with them. "What d'you think you're playing at?"

"Nothing!" Matt shrugged, all innocence. "Me and Tasha were just off to check the railway timetables for her getting back down to London on Monday night. You can't exactly go to the station without going past here, can you?"

He did have a point. The station was about fifty metres from the café and you could hear the station announcer from inside, even with the door shut.

"Yeah, but you could have timed it a bit better!" Ollie jerked his thumb in the direction of the End. "What are you trying to do to Cat, for God's sake?"

Matt glanced over at the window and saw four faces glaring out at him.

"How was I to know Cat would be in the caff?" he said, shrugging his shoulders.

"It wouldn't take a rocket scientist to work out she might be in there, since it's where everyone is, including you, most Saturday mornings! And you—" Ollie turned to his sister. "What are you doing with him, after what happened last night, Tash?"

"Oh, stop coming over all protective brother on me, Ol," Natasha sighed. "Matt explained everything to me..."

"Did he now? Well, I'd be interested to hear that explanation myself," said Ollie, staring daggers at his friend.

"Er, later, Ol," Matt said sheepishly. "Tasha's got some stuff to do in town and I said I'd give her a hand."

Ollie didn't know who to feel more angry with – two-timing Matt or his sister for being so gullible.

"You I want to speak to later, right?" said Ollie, poking Matt in the chest, aware that he should get back to the café and not leave Anna on her own for too long. He hadn't even shown her how to work the ancient coffee machine yet.

"Er, right," muttered Matt, beginning to look slightly guilty.

"Give it a rest, Ol," said Natasha in a bored drawl. "I'm a big girl – I know what I'm doing."

"I doubt it," quipped Ollie, turning away from his sister and heading back to the End. Ever since she'd started modelling, no one could tell her anything – she always knew best.

Fuming, Ollie barged back into the café, grabbed a tray and immediately started clearing tables.

He should have known he wasn't going to get away with it that easily.

"Well?" said Sonja, grabbing his arm as he passed.

"Forget about him. You don't need him," Ollie said bluntly to Catrina. "You could have any bloke you wanted, y'know."

"Yeah? Do you think so?" blinked Cat as tears threatened to spill over yet again.

But even as she dug into her bag for yet another tissue, a plan began to hatch in her mind...

CHAPTER 5

. . . .

REVENGE IS SWEET

Cat was going to make Matt suffer for what he'd done and nobody was going to stop her, of that she was certain. It wasn't exactly the first time she'd been dumped or hurt by a boy, but it was the first time she'd been in love, and only one thing was going to make her feel better. Getting her own back.

Climbing the stairs to the third floor of the mansion block where she lived with her mother, Cat considered the options that had been whirling around her head since she'd seen Matt strut past the End with Natasha on his arm. She found it hard to think of him without feeling a pang. Every time she saw his face in her mind's eye, she remembered how much she'd loved looking at him, loved kissing him, loved the way he smelled.

She paused and leaned against the cool, tiled wall.

Stop thinking like that, she told herself. *I've got to be more focused and less emotional about all this.*

As she turned her key in the door, Cat once again rejected the first idea that had come to her – to destroy Matt's precious record collection.

His records were the real love of his life, as well as being his livelihood *(apart from the sizeable monthly allowance he gets from his daddy dearest*, snorted Cat inwardly). The problem was getting near them. He kept his records locked up in vandal-proof boxes, except for the few he took out at a time when he was DJing.

But, and this was the best but, Cat knew that after his miserable years at boarding school and his lacklustre home life, there was something else that mattered – very much – to Matt. His friends.

"Oh, there you are, Catrina. Where've you been all day? I tried to get you on your mobile – don't you ever take it out with you? Another waste of money, I suppose. I can't understand why you find it so hard to leave me a note to let me know where you are..."

Standing in the hall, Cat stared at her mother,

who was busily juicing a carrot in the kitchen.

"Leave it out, Mum," Cat snapped. After leaving her friends at the café, she'd spent the whole afternoon wandering aimlessly round the clothes shops in the town centre. "At least I'm home sometimes. Unlike some total workaholics who'd rather be in the office or the gym instead of being at home with their children!"

"Don't you *dare* talk to me like that!" barked Sylvia Osgood, her precision-cut bob whipping round as she turned to face her daughter. "I work hard because I *have* to, since I have to pay for you – *and* the mobile phone I gave you and you never use – without *any* support from your father. You should learn some respect and try and help me more, instead of wasting time with those loser friends of Sonja's. And by the way, a couple of them have been on the phone for you. That Maya girl and that Ozzie."

"Ollie, not Ozzie," said Cat, aware that her mother knew full well what her friends' names were. It was as if she did it to be difficult or something.

So Maya and Ollie called, she thought to herself, turning her back on her mother and heading towards the phone in the living room. *I only left them a few hours ago, but they're obviously worried that I'm going to do something stupid, like go round to Matt's and chuck paint over his precious car.*

But Cat had something far more sophisticated in mind for Matt. She was going to make sure that all his friends turned against him.

They'd already been shocked by his actions, that was obvious from last night *and* the way they'd all rallied round her today. It wouldn't take much to make their disgust permanent.

Picking up the phone, Cat dialled The Swan's number.

"Hello?" said a female voice that didn't belong to Ollie's friendly mum.

"Oh, hello, Natasha. Still gracing us with your presence?" said Cat, her heart beating like crazy. Somehow, she hadn't expected her rival to answer the phone.

"Who is this?" said Natasha, momentarily thrown.

"It's Catrina," she drawled in her most pretend-poised way. "Can you get your brother for me, please?"

In the silence that followed, Cat breathed deeply and tried to regain her composure.

"Cat?" came a voice down the line.

"Hi, Ollie – my mum said you called..."

"Yeah, Cat, I just wanted to see if you were OK."

"That's so sweet of you, Ollie. Yes, I'm fine. Don't worry about me."

A thought struck Cat: she'd have to start laying the foundations of her plan. "I mean, I don't want you and Matt falling out over me..."

"Don't be daft, Cat. I mean, I know I'm Matt's mate, but I really don't approve of what he did, y'know."

Cat smiled to herself.

"Well, I'd hate to see everyone taking sides. So I'm going to make the peace. And just to prove it, I'll even go to Matt's party next Saturday."

"Good for you, Cat!" said Ollie.

You'd better believe it's going to be good for me, thought Cat.

CHAPTER 6

● ●

BUSINESS AS USUAL

"I see Madam's got over Matt pretty quickly," sniffed Sonja, watching as Catrina flicked her hair back and giggled with a boy over by the entrance to the main school building. Kerry, who was struggling to pull on a heavy rucksack loaded down with project work, looked up to see what Sonja was talking about.

"Maybe," said Kerry, hauling her bag up on to her shoulder. "But the way she was talking on Saturday, I had visions of Matt's tyres being let down at the dead of night, or his whole house being toilet-papered."

Across the concourse stood Maya. Just out of class, she was looking down at her watch and obviously wondering where her friends were.

Behind her loomed the huge building that comprised the secondary school division of St Mark's, which she and Catrina attended. To the left stood the independent annexe housing the sixth-form college, which Kerry, Sonja and Joe went to.

"Nah, she's obviously over him," huffed Sonja as they strolled over to join Maya. "She's back in full flirt, isn't she?"

"She's talking to that lad about some coursework, if you must know," said Maya defensively, having caught the tail-end of what Sonja was saying. "And anyway, I think it's good if Cat's put it all behind her so quickly. She was pretty humiliated by the whole Natasha business, you know. She might just be putting on a brave face and trying to get on with her life, which – for the sake of the rest of us – is exactly what we all wanted her to do."

Grudgingly, Sonja shrugged and knew her friend was right. "Yeah, I suppose we shouldn't moan. At least there's a chance we might get through the week without any more dramas. What'll happen about Matt's party, though? She's not going to want to turn up to that, is she?"

"Actually, she is," said Maya. "I phoned her on Saturday to see if she was all right and she told me she'd decided to try to forgive and forget, which I think is really brilliant of her."

"What'll Matt make of her coming?" worried Kerry.

"He'd better be on his best behaviour," frowned Maya. "After all, if *Cat's* going to be mature about this..."

"Ha! Cat – mature! More like she knows how popular Matt's parties are and reckons that it's the best chance she's got of copping off with someone new!" snorted Sonja.

Maya glared disapprovingly at Sonja, but didn't say anything. She knew that deep down Sonja and Cat were hugely fond of each other, but the cousins couldn't help sniping at each other and bickering, in an almost sisterly way. In any case, she couldn't say anything because Cat had finished her conversation and was on her way over to join them.

● ● ●

Perched on a stool in the End-of-the-Line café, Matt was trying to explain himself to Ollie.

"So I just told Tasha that I'd been planning to finish with Cat anyway, and that she – well, us – I mean, that kiss on Friday sort of made my mind up. Didn't Tasha tell you any of this?"

"Oh, no. My darling sister told me in no

46

uncertain terms that it was none of my business," said Ollie from his side of the counter. "So what do you mean – *were* you going to finish with Cat? Or did you just tell Tasha that as a handy excuse?"

"No, no – I really meant to finish with her," said Matt, running his hand through his thick dark hair. "It was just a bit tricky, y'know? Finding the right time and all that."

"But why? You never said anything! I thought you two were really into each other!"

"I just – I just think we made a mistake, y'know?" Matt struggled to explain himself. "Friends going out together... it doesn't work. It kinda felt weird, us being together like that."

"Well, something tells me Cat saw it differently," said Ollie.

"Yeah, I know," nodded Matt. "I sort of had an idea she was pretty serious about me and that's why I'd been thinking about knocking it on the head. Y'know, before it got out of hand."

Ollie and Matt looked at each other and found themselves grinning at the irony of what he'd just said.

"Mmm, I'm glad you handled it so well then," said Ollie with good-humoured sarcasm. "Like that tactful moment when you laughed at her when she fell over – after trying to lump you one."

"Oh, I know that was bad, but it was all so ridiculous that I couldn't help it," said Matt, burying his head in his hands with embarrassment. Then he looked up at his friend's face and both boys burst out laughing.

At that moment the bell of the café door tinkled loudly.

"Thanks again for being so brilliant on Saturday," Cat was trilling to the other girls. "I don't know how I'd have survived without you!"

She must have spotted the looks on her friends' faces and turned round to see what they were staring at.

"Oh, God!" groaned Matt only loud enough for Ollie to hear. He knew what it must look like to the girls: him heartlessly cackling when Cat was probably still hurting. And he truly hadn't meant to hurt her; he just hadn't handled it right and hadn't been able to stop himself falling for Ollie's gorgeous sister.

"Er, hi, girls," Matt said nervously, walking over to meet them. He knew he had some serious making up to do. "Catrina, can I have a chat with you some time? Y'know, about everything?"

"Yeah, I suppose so," she said quietly, her eyes fixed on the ground. "Now?"

"Er, I can't just now," Matt mumbled, his handsome face looking ever-so-slightly red. "I've got to, er, go somewhere..."

"Where?" asked Sonja bluntly. Laughing like he didn't have a care in the world was one thing, but now he had the perfect opportunity to make peace with Cat and he was faffing around!

"I'm sorry, I – I've got to, erm, go and pick up Tasha in a minute. I said I'd give her a lift back down to the station..." said Matt, looking acutely embarrassed by now.

Everyone – including Matt – fell silent, waiting for Catrina to have hysterics. But she just looked him in the eye, smiled sweetly and said, "Well, *do* give her another birthday kiss from me, Matt!" before pushing past him and taking a seat at an empty table.

"Matt, you're an idiot," snarled Sonja before going over to join Catrina. Maya and Kerry gave him despairing looks and followed suit.

Over by the counter, Ollie was scribbling down an order from a customer. He pulled an 'omigod' face at his friend.

I've really, really messed this one up, Matt groaned to himself as he fled from the café.

CHAPTER 7

• •

THREE DOWN, TWO TO GO

The following Saturday morning Cat woke up with a smile on her face. She ran over the events of the last week in her head. Everything had happened much more easily than she'd expected, but then she hadn't anticipated Matt playing right into her hands on Monday in the café.

The girls had been furious with him. Not only had they caught him laughing like a drain, but he'd blown Cat out for Natasha *again*. All week long, they'd been going over and over his bad behaviour and there'd even been talk of boycotting the party. But Cat had insisted.

"I don't want to be the cause of breaking the crowd up!" she'd protested in her best martyred voice. "And I want to go to show him – to show him he hasn't got to me!"

Kerry, Maya and even cynical Sonja had been impressed at the way she was handling it all. And so they were going to Matt's party.

Cat stretched and yawned in the sunlight streaming through her bedroom window, anticipating the moment she would get the chance to show off The Dress.

She gazed at it from her bed, its long, slinky black shape draped over a hanger on her wardrobe door. Slashed to the thigh and plunging at the neck, it gave her curves upon her curves – a killer dress that was going to make heads turn like spectators at Wimbledon.

And a certain head in particular was going to turn tonight, which was the real reason why she wanted to go to the party tonight...

The girls had been easy, a walkover; female bonding meant that they took her side against Matt as a matter of course. Her real problem had been working out how to turn Joe and Ollie against their mate.

Ollie had been all too keen to try and put Matt's case forward, telling the girls how sorry he was. And while Ollie still felt some loyalty to Matt, Joe did too – he always took Ollie's lead, doing whatever Ollie did. *Like a little shadow*, thought Cat.

So Cat had got her brain into gear to do some

serious thinking. And she had come up with an inspired scheme: she was going to go out with Ollie.

It was perfect. Having Ollie as a boyfriend meant he would *have* to be on her side, and it would drive a nice little wedge between Ollie and Matt, especially if she ended up getting off with him at Matt's party. All his friends turning against him (because Joe would switch sides in a minute if Ollie told him to) and public humiliation at his own party. Double whammy.

Mmm, this revenge game is going to be fun, Cat smiled to herself.

• • •

While Catrina was gloating, Kerry was fretting. And shopping in town with Sonja.

"So Elaine's maybe coming for the party tonight?"

"Yeah, so Ollie says. But she didn't bother coming to his birthday do last week, so I don't see why she'd make the effort for this one," shrugged Sonja, rifling through a rack of tops in Miss Selfridge.

Kerry couldn't really get her head round Ollie and his 'girlfriend'. Elaine was this hippy, space cadet of a girl he'd met a few months before at a music festival in a country park. Kerry couldn't remember now why she and the others hadn't gone to it, but Joe and Ollie had, and Elaine had been a fixture ever since.

"What's the matter, are you jealous or something?" Sonja had teased her once when they'd been discussing Ollie and Elaine's long-distance friendship. (He'd insisted it wasn't love, though they'd all ganged up on Joe one night and got him to admit that Ollie and Elaine had ended up snogging that first time they'd met.)

"No!" Kerry had protested at the time. "It's just confusing – are they going out or what?"

No one knew for sure and Ollie was infuriatingly vague about Elaine. Sometimes she'd travel over from her town to see him and hang out with the gang – probably unaware of the way they studied her and Ollie's body language for clues – and then not be seen again for ages.

It made Kerry nervous. She liked things to be as straightforward as possible. Which was another reason why this bust-up with Matt and Catrina was stressing her out.

As they made their way out of the store, Kerry started to cheer up slightly. She was going to make a huge effort tonight and was determined to look beautiful.

Well, beautiful-ish. She'd just bought some

pale blue, sparkly nail varnish and Sonja was lending her some black suede, high-heeled boots. She might even try and manage without her glasses for once. All she needed now was an outfit.

"How about that, Kerry?" Sonja suggested, pointing to a dress in the window of a shop they were passing. "It would look brilliant on you!"

"Don't be silly, Son. That's the sort of thing Cat wears," Kerry scowled, eyeing the figure-hugging, black lace number with great suspicion. It wasn't her at all. She'd just feel exposed and lumpy in something like that. She needed something that she'd feel confident in.

Like a bin bag, Kerry thought to herself.

In fact, she'd already spotted a midnight blue shirt she really liked the look of. It was slightly glittery and made from a soft, satiny material, and she knew it would suit her, especially if she wore it with her black hipsters, which definitely went well with the boots. The only problem was, she'd seen it in the window of a tacky boutique normally frequented by mums and she wasn't sure what super-cool Sonja would have to say about that.

"Erm, look, Son... you don't have to stick with me all afternoon. You know what a pain I am about choosing clothes..."

"You're not wrong there."

"Yeah, so why don't we split up now and I'll come round and get changed at yours later on."

"OK," said Sonja, already drifting off to examine something that had caught her eye in a window. "See you about eight then."

• • •

Kerry stashed the bag from the deeply untrendy boutique inside another one, just in case she bumped into Sonja. It wasn't that she was scared of her friend's judgement – she just knew she'd never hear the last of it. Sonja could be merciless about certain things.

Yeah, well it's all right for her, thought Kerry grimly. *She never has to worry about looking good.*

Glancing up, she spotted a familiar face among the shoppers. Thankfully, it wasn't Sonja's.

"Joe! Hi, what are you up to?"

"Hello Kerry. Um... nothing much. Bumming about. Ollie's, y'know, working."

Joe blushed furiously. He was useless at talking to girls. Even girls who were supposed to be his friends. He often wished he had some of Ollie's easy-going charm, but knew it was never going to happen. They'd hung about together since they were little and it had always been the same – Ollie doing the meeting and greeting, Joe bumbling along in the background.

"Yes, of course," nodded Kerry, thinking of Ollie slaving away on this busy Saturday lunchtime with only Dorothy – one of the two old ladies who helped out at the End – to help. She and Sonja had stuck their heads round the café door as they wandered into town and heard Ollie moan about his Uncle Nick doing another disappearing trick when it was supposed to be his shift. Nick was good at that.

"Yeah..." said Joe, his side of the conversation grinding to a halt.

He had a bit of a problem knowing what to say to Kerry, mainly because he had a soft spot for her. No, more than a soft spot. And it made him clam up completely when he found himself alone with her like this.

"I meant to say, Joe," Kerry smiled at him, making his heart thunder, "I can't believe that was your first gig the other night at Ollie's party. You were brilliant!"

"Really?" Joe managed to smile back, now glowing with pride as well as embarrassment.

"God, yeah. I mean, I missed most of it because I was on toilet duty – you know, sorting Cat out. But I could hear every song from in there.

That really sad one you did was my favourite. Was it a Verve song? It sounded like it..."

Joe shook his head – he couldn't speak. It was the only song that hadn't been a cover. In fact, he'd written it himself.

Now he really was in love with Kerry.

CHAPTER 8

• •

PARTY PARTY

"Kerry, Sonja, all right? Come in... Nice dress, Sonny – I might just have to snog you later!"

Matt froze, reminding himself that things weren't back to normal with the girls and he couldn't just joke around like he used to – not yet, anyway.

"Sorry, Matt, no snogs from me," retorted Sonja. "Remember how much trouble you got into last time you decided to snog a gorgeous blonde?"

Chastised, Matt nodded and shut the door behind them.

"Are the others here yet?" Sonja asked.

From the noises coming from the basement it sounded as if the party was already in full swing. *Maybe it's a good sign,* she thought.

Matt nodded. "Yeah – the lads have been here for a while and Maya and, er, Cat arrived about five minutes ago. They're in the loo, I think."

Sonja got on pretty well with Matt on the whole. He could be such a smoothie sometimes, you had to laugh at him.

He was so cocky, it was sometimes hard to believe there was a human heart beating underneath that gorgeous exterior, but Sonja liked him none the less.

And it occurred to her that maybe they'd all punished him enough over this little episode.

"Sounds busy down there, Matt," said Kerry, wriggling out of her jacket.

As the girls made their way down the stairs into Matt's famous den, they stopped to read the orange fluorescent graffiti emblazoned on the walls. There were pens dangling on strings from the ceiling so everyone could leave their Day-Glo messages.

Matt had rigged up a new ultraviolet light so the words really showed up. It also gave everyone bluish-white eyes and teeth, and Sonja and Kerry turned to pull scary goblin faces at each other.

"I like your top, Kez," said Sonja, her face back to normal. "Where'd you get it from?"

"Oh, um, I just remembered about it when I was going round the shops – Mum got it for me a few weeks ago. It was a surprise to, er, thank me for babysitting Lewis so much recently..."

"That's funny, I could've sworn I saw that very shirt in the window of Jean's Jeans..."

"I don't think so, Son. She, er, said she bought it the last time she was in the city. Maybe you saw something similar..."

Kerry stared at Sonja as she headed off to fetch a bowl of tortilla chips. How did Sonja always manage to make her feel inferior?

And why did Kerry let her? She *knew* she looked nice tonight.

Well... perhaps not great by Sonja's standards, but certainly a lot prettier than usual.

Kerry really wanted to go the whole hog and be glasses free tonight, and now that they were safely inside, what could happen to her?

She made up her mind. The glasses were coming off.

Discreetly stashing the offending specs in her mini rucksack, Kerry was instantly plunged into Blursville. Everything around her became woolly and indistinct and Kerry suddenly felt a bit wobbly.

Holding her hand against the wall to steady herself, she was relieved to hear a familiar voice behind her.

"Kez! All right? You look nice – new shirt?"

Ollie was wearing a bright yellow Scooby Doo T-shirt, green combats and very grubby trainers. But he looked good. Ollie always looked good somehow, whatever he threw on.

"Elaine here?" she asked him, peering around for the familiar extensions and the glint of a nose ring.

"Nah – she phoned to say she's too skint to come over at the moment."

"Oh, I'm sorry, Ol..."

"Sorry?" Ollie smiled quizzically at her. "Don't be sorry! It's only E! I'll catch up with her some time."

A commotion on the stairs made them break off their conversation. It was Catrina – fresh from a make-up retouch – making her grand entrance. In the raunchiest dress ever invented.

Her bleached blonde hair hung in film star ringlets and she'd apparently applied her make-up with a trowel.

She looked pretty amazing, there was no denying it, but even Kerry in her short-sighted haze could see that Cat's look was *completely* over the top. And so was her behaviour – just like old times.

"Ollie! Come and look what I've written on the wall. Haaaah! It's a bit rude, actually..." cackled Catrina, pretending to look ashamed.

"Better go and see what she's up to!" said Ollie, rolling his eyes.

Suddenly launched back into the loneliness of Blursville, Kerry was relieved when Joe appeared at her side.

"Kerry... er, d'you want a, um, peanut or something?"

"No, I'm fine thanks, Joe," she blinked at him.

Joe shuffled a bit, wondering where to go from here. He cleared his throat and was about to try again when Sonja and Maya joined them.

"Come on, Maya," Sonja was saying, "even you have to admit that Cat's not just putting on a brave face tonight."

"Hmm," nodded Maya, watching Cat's antics.

Joe glanced over to the foot of the stairs to see what the girls were on about. Catrina was letting rip with another raucous cackle, one arm draped around Ollie, the other hand theatrically covering her cleavage as she shook with laughter.

All the lads in the room had their eyes glued to her.

Ollie, meanwhile, was chuffed to see Catrina in such good form.

"I know I'm going to have a good time tonight, Ollie. 'Specially with great mates like you around," she smiled at him.

Ollie hugged her.

"Atta girl, Cat! Forget all about Matt – just stick with me and we'll have a right laugh!"

Well, thought Cat, *if that's not encouragement, I don't know what is! Ollie Stanton, you are not going to know what's hit you.*

CHAPTER 9

● ●

CAT POUNCES

As the party livened up and the dancing got going, Sonja and Kerry joined in. Kerry always hated those first few moments on the dance floor. Sonja, of course, was a supremely confident dancer; Kerry always took a while to warm up. She loved dancing, but she couldn't help feeling self-conscious while her legs and hips jerked around as they struggled to find the rhythm.

Six tracks on, Maya motioned the other two girls over and all three flopped into the newly vacated beanbags in the far corner of Matt's den.

"Ooh, this feels nice!" said Sonja, sinking back on the rustly cushions. "My shoes are killing me – I knew I should have worn my trainers!"

"How's Cat managing? Have you seen the size of her *heels*?" joked Maya.

"We noticed all right," nodded Sonja. "Speaking of Cat, have you seen her around?"

"I saw her upstairs in the lounge a few minutes ago, giggling away with Ollie about something," said Maya.

"What's she up to?" Kerry frowned. "She hasn't left him for a minute all night!"

"Yeah, we were watching her earlier when we lost you and Joe," Sonja explained to Maya. "She was chasing Ollie all over the party and he was just laughing it off. He wasn't exactly telling her where to go, although I bet he wants to. Probably too worried about hurting her feelings, knowing Ol."

"I think she's on a mission," sighed Maya. "You know, trying to show Matt how little she's bothered about him. And Ollie's the perfect person for her to party with."

The girls nodded. Maya was probably right. She usually was.

"So, anyway, I meant to ask – any idea who wrote that obscene poem on Matt's graffiti wall?"

Sonja and Kerry groaned and said "Guess!" in unison.

"And do we know if the graffiti artist has had any kind of proper apology from Matt yet?" Maya asked.

"Not that we've heard. Maybe Joe'll know.

He's over there, looking lost as usual," said Sonja, pointing to where Joe was standing.

In fact, lost was the last thing Joe was feeling. He was right where he wanted to be – in a spot where he could surreptitiously watch Kerry.

"Hey, Joey, siddown!" yelled Sonja, waving him over. "Wanna join our bitchy conversation? C'mon, tell us something funny..."

As Joe sat down next to Kerry he blushed a deep shade of crimson. Kerry groaned inwardly. Everyone knew Joe was painfully shy and it was mean of Sonja to draw attention to him like this. It was almost like bullying him, especially when he was the last person in the world with the confidence to entertain all three of them.

"Don't worry, Joe – you don't need to start dredging up knock-knock jokes," said Kerry, smiling at him reassuringly. "We only wanted to ask if Matt's got round to apologising to Cat yet."

"Not that I know of," he shrugged, aiming his words at Kerry and Kerry alone. She always knew how to make him feel at his ease. That was one of the reasons he liked her so much.

Encouraged, Joe leaned forward to say something else. But nothing came out. Then, in a flash of inspiration, he remembered some advice he'd read in a magazine: *If you can't think of anything to say, ask the person about herself...*

"That shirt... it's... it suits you. Where's it from?"

Now it was Kerry's turn to blush. She was desperate for Sonja not to start on about that stupid shirt again. Kerry knew she'd never ever hear the last of it.

"Oh, this– this old thing. I've had it for ages," Kerry said abruptly and turned away from him to Sonja and Maya. "Do you want a drink of anything? Coke, Maya?"

Joe was aghast. What had he done wrong? Girls liked talking about their clothes, didn't they? According to that magazine, he'd said exactly the right thing to start a conversation, yet Kerry had just changed the subject. He felt even more hopeless.

"Er, I'll come with you and give you a hand, if you like, Kerry... if that's OK," he blustered, trying to do something right.

Kerry nodded. She was grateful for the company. She knew she was a hazard and bound to fall over or walk into something if left to her own myopic devices.

Joe smiled and felt a bit happier. Being useful was good. Being useful was at least a start.

• • •

Cat stared at her reflection in the bathroom mirror and sighed. Her plan wasn't working.

She'd been flirting her heart out for three hours now and Ollie wasn't getting the message at all. Part of the problem was of her own making, she knew. Like the boy who cried wolf, Cat had *always* flirted with Ollie, but it was just fun stuff that never meant anything. Now that it *was* supposed to mean something, she couldn't blame Ollie for assuming she was just being her usual, full-on, flippant self.

Even plying him with lager hadn't helped. She'd figured that with a few beers inside him, his defences might come down and she could charm him into her arms more easily. But several bottles later (he hadn't seemed to notice that every time Cat got him a drink, she didn't get one for herself), Ollie wasn't so much amorous as legless.

She'd even dragged him away from the party downstairs and pulled him into the lounge for a bit of privacy, but Ollie seemed more interested in playing with Matt's dad's state-of-the-art TV than cuddling up on the sofa.

"Come on, Cat," she told her reflection, "you'll never get a better chance to do this. You've got to think of something!"

"Oi! 'Urry up in there!" a male voice slurred from the other side of the door.

"Shut it!" Cat yelled back. That's what she hated about parties – the way lads who were potentially cute at the start of the night turned into drunken oafs by the end.

Giving her hair a final tweak, Cat was about to head back to her own drunken oaf in the lounge when inspiration struck.

She'd come up with Plan B: she was going to go for the sympathy vote.

• • •

"Aw, great, you're back. I just wanted to show you this – listen to the stereo speakers on this baby!" Ollie said over his shoulder, pointing the remote at the TV.

Cat winced as the screech of a movie car chase belted out at ear-splitting volume.

She shook herself and composed her features into a look of abject misery.

"Oh, Ollie!" she said in a frail little voice.

Ollie, slightly worse for wear, was transfixed by the widescreen picture in front of him.

"Oh, Ollie!" Cat repeated.

Her voice was still too feeble to be heard above the shooting that had now started. Cat sighed and walked in-between Ollie and the TV and tried again.

"Oh, Ollie!"

She looked the picture of misery. Ollie quickly fumbled with the remote and pressed the off button.

"What's wrong?" he asked, full of concern.

"Oh Ollie, it's so awful! I can't believe what Matt's been saying..."

"What? What's he been saying?"

"He's been telling people I–, that I–, I *slept* with him!" she choked out. "It's not true, Ollie!"

Catrina started sobbing, her shoulders shaking.

"He's been what? Nah! Matt wouldn't do that..."

"Well, that's not what I just heard!"

Ollie was aghast. "Cat, calm down a minute. Are you sure about this? How do you know he's been saying this stuff?"

Between sobs and gulps, Catrina got her story out.

"I was in the loo just now and I heard these two lads talking outside the door. They were going on about what a laugh Matt was, 'specially that story about how he 'got what he wanted' from some girl before he dumped her. It was only when they started talking about the girl and how she was somewhere at the party that I suddenly realised they were describing *me*!"

"Are you sure they were talking about you, Cat?" asked Ollie, finding it hard to believe Matt would be so callous.

"Oh, yes – they said the one with the blonde hair and the sexy dress and the big..." Catrina didn't finish the sentence, but glanced down at her chest.

"Who were these guys, Cat?" asked Ollie.

"I don't know. I didn't recognise their voices," she sniffed and shook her head. "And I was too mortified to come out of the loo until I heard them move away."

"I just can't understand why Matt'd do—"

"He obviously just did it to hurt me – to get back at me for laying into him at your party! And spreading lies about having sex is the easiest way to hurt me, isn't it?"

"Aw, c'mere," said Ollie, reaching out and pulling Cat into his arms protectively.

Cat faked a few more sobs into his shoulder, while secretly congratulating herself on a successful scam. OK, so she hadn't managed to get Ollie to fall for her, or at least snog her in front of Matt, but this would do nicely. Ollie (and soon Joe in tow) wouldn't be able to forgive Matt for rubbishing a friend like that. No way.

"Listen, Cat," said Ollie, leaning back a little and gazing into her tear-filled eyes, "you're a

71

lovely girl and no one who cares about you will believe that stuff. I certainly don't."

His arms wrapped comfortingly around her, his kind, sweet face only inches away, Cat was suddenly aware that Plan A might still be an option after all...

Leaning imperceptibly towards Ollie, she heard him let out a tiny gasp of surprise just before her lips touched his.

CHAPTER 10

• •

UH-OH...

Ollie woke with a pounding headache and a gentle thumping on the arm from his dad.

"Rise and shine, Sleeping Beauty! You've got a date with your nan, remember?'

"Wha–?" Ollie couldn't even form words, his mouth felt so dry. His tongue seemed huge and was stuck uncomfortably to the roof of his mouth.

"Nice pyjamas," said his dad, nodding at the Scooby Doo T-shirt and combats that his son was still wearing.

Ollie wiggled his toes under the duvet and realised he still had his trainers on too.

"Here, your mum thought I should bring you up a cup of tea. Although why either of us should be nice to you after the racket you made coming in so late, I don't know."

Ollie struggled up to a sitting position and noticed that his dad was grinning and holding a steaming mug. He lurched towards it and his dad laughed.

"Ooh, you are in a state, aren't you, mate? Better get yourself in that shower. We're having Sunday lunch with your nan, in case you'd forgotten, and I don't want her to be shocked by the state of her beloved grandson."

"Oh, Dad, couldn't we—"

"Don't even start," said Stuart Stanton, looking at his son with mock sternness. "No, we *can't* make it another time because your nan's made you a belated birthday cake 'specially and, since your sister's not around, it's my job to see that at least one of her grandchildren turns up and says thank you nicely."

Ollie slurped his tea as if his life depended on it. Luckily, he got on pretty well with his dad so he knew he wasn't in serious trouble over last night's drunken behaviour, although he realised he'd better not make a habit of it.

But more worrying than that were the fragmented memories that came drifting back bit by bit from the night before.

Matt's party... beer... him and Joe carrying boxes of CDs... Kerry's glittery eye shadow... a very rude poem on the wall... Catrina giggling...

dancing to Abba (Abba!)... more beer... Catrina crying... Catrina...

"Omigod!" groaned Ollie and collapsed back on to his pillows.

• • •

As the day wore on, Ollie started to feel seriously guilty.

His nan fussed around him, all apologies for having had too bad a cold to make it to his party the previous week. To compensate, she'd made so much food that the table groaned under its weight; food that – in Ollie's present hung-over state – he couldn't do justice to.

She'd popped a surprisingly big cheque inside his birthday card too, so he could start buying the parts he needed for the second-hand Vespa his folks had bought him. His mum and dad kept teasing him about his hangover, but had obviously forgiven him.

Everyone was being so nice, but he didn't deserve it. Not him. Not someone who could drunkenly snog his friend.

Why did I do it? How could I have done that to Cat when she was feeling so vulnerable? he groaned to himself for the hundredth time. *How could I have taken advantage of her like that?*

"Here we are, Ollie, your favourite pudding," beamed his nan, cutting him a giant slice of strawberry and cream layer cake.

He smiled weakly and wondered how to force it down. As he lifted a forkful to his mouth, his gaze fell on an overflowing vase of burgundy tulips and he was instantly reminded of Cat again. Of those dark red lips coming up to meet his....

"Uhhhhh."

"What is it, Ollie love? Still not feeling too clever?" fussed his nan, interpreting Ollie's low moan as another sign of over-indulgence from the night before. "I'll fetch you an aspirin."

She may have misinterpreted the actual reason, but his grandmother was right about him not feeling too clever. Ollie felt downright stupid.

He had meant to try and heal the rift in the crowd after the Catrina and Matt fiasco; and he'd also meant to help Cat cheer up. Not get off with her.

If things were messy before, they were a hell of a lot messier now.

• • •

Catrina spent her Sunday curled up in bed in a funny mood. She warmed up some of yesterday's pizza. She watched soap opera after soap opera after crummy old *Carry On* film. She took a long, hot, bubbly bath, slathered on a face pack and played all her favourite CDs. But she still felt down.

Everything worked – better than I'd hoped, she thought to herself, lying back on her bed and aimlessly twirling a CD round on her finger. *After last night, no one's going to go near Matt again. So why do I feel so weird?*

She already knew the answer, but she didn't exactly relish it. Ollie was one of the nicest guys she knew. A real sweetie with a heart of gold. A total mate. And here she was using him.

As for snogging him... instead of the tummy-tingling, heart-thumping sensation she'd got whenever she kissed Matt, there was, well, nothing. In fact, after their kiss, Ollie had looked positively ill, which she knew was down to the amount of alcohol he'd drunk, rather than his response to kissing her. At least she hoped it was.

With Ollie in such a state, she hadn't been able to continue their snogging session anywhere in Matt's view; all she could do was roll Ollie out of the door – via a tumble over some empty beer crates in the hall – into the fresh air and all the way to his front door.

"Catrina," her mother's voice jarred her from her thoughts. "I do wonder if half past four isn't a little late to be getting up, even by your standards. Do you think you could make it through to the living room for a phone call? It's that Ozzie again."

Ignoring the sarcasm in her mother's voice, Cat swung herself off the bed and made her way to the phone.

"Cat, it's Ollie."

"Ollie! Hi!" she said brightly.

"I just rang to see if you're, um, OK."

"Well, I'm still pretty upset about—" Cat leant over and shut the door on her prying mother "—you know, what Matt was saying. But you certainly helped to cheer me up..."

"Um, well, good. Listen – I'm in a bit of a rush; I've got some stuff to do. But I'll catch up with you down the End some time this week, yeah?"

"Yeah. That would be nice," purred Cat.

As she put the phone down, Catrina knew that the weird feeling she'd had all day was guilt. Guilt at using and abusing her friend.

But what can I do? she shrugged to herself. *I can't let go of my advantage. Matt's going to suffer when he realises everyone hates him and he's going to suffer even more seeing me and Ollie together.*

CHAPTER 11

● ●

PARTY POST-MORTEM

"I tell you, he was looking at you!"

"No, he wasn't!"

"Was."

"Wasn't!"

"Was."

"Oh, shut up, Sonja. You know boys don't look at me when they've got you to lust after."

"WAS, WASN'T! WAS, WASN'T! WAS, WASN—"

"And you can shut up too, Lewis," said Kerry, giving her little brother a harder push on the swing.

"How would you know who was or wasn't looking at you?" said Sonja, swinging idly on the seat next to Lewis. "You couldn't see a thing last night. You're blind as a bat without your glasses."

Kerry didn't have the energy to argue back: babysitting Lewis after the late night they'd had was a bit too much to handle. And Sonja wasn't much use. Instead of helping to entertain Lewis, she was more interested in trying to convince Kerry that Mick, the bass player in The Loud, had been giving Kerry the eye while they were all on the dance floor.

Unable to believe that *anyone* would fancy her, Kerry couldn't help but wonder if this was just Sonja's way of taking her mind off the fact that Ollie had last been seen heading out of the door of Matt's house, drunk out of his skull, with Cat draped around him – and Cat's lipstick smeared across his face.

Both girls knew that this was just more bad news for the future harmony of their crowd and Sonja guessed, quite rightly, that Kerry was fretting about it. But then Kerry was usually fretting about something.

"Anyway, Mick or no Mick, it was still a laugh last night, wasn't it?" asked Sonja, looking at her friend with some concern.

"Sure," Kerry answered flatly.

Sonja stopped swinging and looked at her friend.

"Kerry, Ollie won't go out with Cat, y'know. He was just drunk and being silly."

"Who was drunk?" asked Lewis.

"No one. Now shut up or I won't buy you any Monster Munch," said Kerry, glaring at the back of her little brother's head.

"YES!" shrieked Lewis and shut up.

"Ollie's not stupid, Kerry. He'll handle it."

"I hope so, for his sake. And ours," mumbled Kerry. "Do you think Matt knows what happened?"

"I don't know," shrugged Sonja. "Maybe Joe spoke to him later, after he came and told us what he saw."

"Maybe," Kerry nodded, looking forlorn. "But I just wish none of this had happened. In fact, I wish Catrina and Matt had never got together in the first place and then we'd all just be mates like we were. Plain and simple."

"I know, but what's done is done. It's not worth worrying about."

"I know, I know," nodded Kerry, aware that Sonja was trying to make it all sound easier than it was, for her sake.

She appreciated the effort and tried to sound brighter than she really felt. "Of course, if Mick *was* looking at me, I wouldn't complain for a second. He's well cute!"

"Yes, he is," Sonja grinned at her.

"And you know what – I might just have to do

something about it!" said Kerry confidently.

"Yeah? Like what?"

"Oh, I dunno. I'll have to see. Maybe I'll ring him up and ask him out, bold as you like."

"Good idea, Kez."

"Yep and then a flock of pigs will fly past the window, and diamonds will rain down from the sky!"

Sonja laughed. She loved the way Kerry could laugh at herself, even though sometimes she wished her ditzy friend was a bit more confident.

"When am I getting my Monster Munch?" came a small voice.

● ● ●

After he put down the phone to Cat, Ollie let out a deep breath then began to dial Joe's number.

"Hey, Joe!"

"Hi, Ol. You OK?"

"Yeah, kind of. Did you have a good time last night?"

Joe's heart started beating like crazy. Had Ollie noticed him drooling over Kerry? He'd always kept his feelings undercover from everyone – even his oldest, closest friend. He took a chance and hoped Ollie didn't mean what he dreaded he meant.

"Um, not really. No, it was rubbish actually."

Joe wasn't lying. Things had gone no further with Kerry (inevitably) and he'd been pretty disturbed at seeing the state Ollie was in, and with what seemed to be happening between him and Catrina.

"Er, how come?" asked Ollie, struggling to remember the details of the previous evening.

"Just this and that," said Joe vaguely. "So, what happened to you, then?"

"Don't ask," Ollie winced. "Well, you can if you like. It's doing my head in, if you must know. Mind if I come over?"

"Sure. I mean, course not. Hang on a minute, Mum's yelling something..." said Joe, as a fuzzy conversation took place in the background. "She's just asked me if you want to come over for your tea."

Ollie sighed. Joe's mum *always* earwigged his phone conversations. It wasn't as if Ollie didn't like the woman, but all he wanted to do right now was talk to his best mate, in private, and get a few things straight in his head.

"Yeah, OK then," Ollie agreed, knowing that, like his nan's strawberry layer cake earlier, there was no getting out of this one. "So long as it's not toad-in-the-hole again."

Ten minutes later, Ollie closed the door that led up to the flat above The Swan, crossed the road and knocked on the front door of the little terraced house where Joe and his mum lived.

"Ollie!" squealed Joe's mum. "Lovely to see you! Tea'll be ready soon, but you can go and play in Joe's room till then!"

Ollie winced. Susie Gladwin was hugely protective of her son and always treated him as if he was about ten years old – and Ollie too. But he managed a smile and went on up to Joe's room, where he found his friend engrossed in some new PlayStation game.

"Check this out – you'll love it," said Joe, not taking his eyes off the screen.

Joe thrashed him four times at the new game before Ollie finally brought up the subject of the previous night.

"So, did I make a bit of a berk of myself at the party then?"

"You tell me," Joe shrugged. "I'm not the one who snogged Cat."

"Oh God... why did I drink so much?" Ollie groaned, covering his face with his hands. "I can hardly remember anything that happened last night!"

"So, you don't remember snogging her?"

"Kind of... But how do you know, Joe?"

"Seeing her lipstick smeared all over your face gave me a bit of a clue. And seeing you staggering out the door with her."

"But you don't know what was going on, Joe!" said Ollie, trying to excuse himself. "She heard this really bad stuff... Matt was telling anyone who'd listen that he'd slept with her!"

"Nah!" said Joe, looking seriously surprised. "Matt wouldn't do that... even if it was true!"

"It's *not* true!" said Ollie, overcome with chivalry. Anything to distract from his own embarrassment. "And Matt definitely said it!"

"How can you be so sure?" Joe replied dubiously. "You don't seem to be sure *what* went on last night..."

"No, Cat told me! That's why she got so upset! That's why I ended up, well, y'know, kissing her and everything..."

"The way I remember it, Cat was stuck to you like a limpet all night. She followed you around the whole time and you were far too trashed to resist anything she sprang on you."

"It wasn't like that!" said Ollie, surprised at Joe's response. "Cat was really upset and vulnerable, 'cause of what Matt said!"

"I think you should speak to Matt before you

do anything else," said Joe, not wanting to fall out with Ollie, but not wishing to take everything at face value either.

Joe might not say that much at times, but it didn't mean he wasn't watching and taking things in. And right now, he wasn't sure *what* was going on in Cat's head.

"And I think you should get things sorted with Cat too – you're just friends, no complications. Right?"

For someone who'd never been out with a girl in his entire life, Joe could be pretty wise when it came to other people's relationships.

"Yeah, you're right," nodded Ollie.

"Anyway, I wanted to let you hear something," said Joe, changing the subject. He turned and picked up the acoustic guitar he kept beside his computer desk and strummed through the chords of the new song that was running through his head.

"That's brilliant, Joe – what's it called?" enthused Ollie.

"*Hopeless*. It's about... It's about someone I met once."

"Yeah? Still, maybe it's a bit slow. What about trying to come up with something more up-beat? We could do with some fast ones in the set."

Slightly dispirited, Joe put the guitar down.

Anyway, it reminded him, once again, of his chances with Kerry. *Hopeless*.

Just then, Joe's mum's shrill tones rang up the stairs like a downmarket and much younger version of Hyacinth Bucket.

"Boys? Joe! Ollie! Come and get iiiiit!"

Joe grinned ruefully at Ollie and the pair trotted dutifully downstairs.

"Mmmmm, toad-in-the-hole! My favourite!" Ollie grinned enthusiastically, trying hard not to look at Joe.

CHAPTER 12

• •

OLLIE WANTS THE TRUTH

Matt was busy cleaning up the den when Ollie arrived. It was Monday, but Matt hadn't felt any rush to get the place straight from the party. His dad was usually away on business, so Matt always had time to get rid of the debris before he returned. And since most of the partying and mess was confined to the den, it wouldn't have troubled his dad anyway.

"Can I give you a hand, Matt? Pass us one of those bin bags..." said Ollie, having let himself in through the open kitchen door.

"Thanks, Ol," smiled Matt, pleased to see his friend. "Not working today?"

"Nah, day off," said Ollie, pulling a tangle of silly string off the back of a chair. "Actually, this isn't the only mess I came to clear up..."

"Yeah? What have I done now?"

Ollie looked at Matt. Did he know that the rumour he'd spread had reached his friends? And did he know what had happened between Ollie and Cat?

"Have you spoken to any of the crowd since the party?" Ollie asked.

"Nope," said Matt. "I haven't been in touch with anyone – I just thought I'd cool it for a bit till everything died down. I was just glad everyone turned up on Saturday night..."

"Well, you're not doing a great deal to help the situation if you go around spreading trashy rumours about people," said Ollie sternly. He was secretly relieved to realise that Matt obviously didn't know about his own little indiscretion yet. And, for the moment, Ollie wasn't about to set the record straight.

"What am I supposed to have said?"

"That stuff about Cat."

"*What* stuff about Cat?"

Ollie was slightly perturbed. Matt did look genuinely confused and clueless on the subject.

"Y'know – about 'getting what you wanted from her' before you 'dumped' her!"

"*Eh!?*"

"Boasting about having sex with her, you idiot!" Ollie shouted angrily at Matt, although a lot of the anger currently coursing through his veins was aimed at himself.

"I never had sex with Cat!"

"I know you didn't – so why were you telling people you did?"

"Ollie, I swear, I've never said anything like that to anyone! Where did you *get* this from?!"

"It– it doesn't matter where it came from," said Ollie, keen to protect Cat from any further complications. "What matters is *why* you said it."

Matt looked seriously annoyed and seemed to be gritting his teeth in an effort to control his temper.

"Look, Ollie, I admit I've been a bit of a selfish prat – showing Cat up like that at your party then rubbing her nose in it when I went past the café with Tasha and everything, but I wouldn't spread stuff like that about! I'm not *that* low!"

"Well, why were some lads going on about it?"

"God, how do I know? Someone's got their wires crossed somewhere."

"It didn't sound that way..."

"Listen, if you don't want to tell me where you got this from then I can't really help sort it out, can I? All I can say is whoever heard it heard wrong."

"OK, OK!" said Ollie, holding up his hands. "I believe you. But the girls are going to be furious when they hear about this, Matt. They're probably all down at the End talking about it now. All I'm saying is you'd better talk to Cat and get this cleared up, unless you want to wear the next cappuccino you come in for."

"But I didn't do—"

"Save it, Matt," Ollie interrupted. "It's not *me* you've got to convince."

The two boys stared at each other in silence for a second, then a cheeky grin spread across Matt's face.

"So, anyway," he said, "has that gorgeous sister of yours been asking about me when she phones home?"

"No, she has not!" laughed Ollie, glad that something had broken the tension, even if it was just Matt being his usual big-headed self.

• • •

"Hey, girls! Where's the funeral?!" cackled Nick, standing with his hands on his hips, beer belly bulging over his white apron, and observing the four miserable-looking people in front of him. "You lot remind me of Tina Turner's backing singers the time they lost the bags with all their stage costumes in. Boy, were they down! I just said to them—"

Nick stopped in mid-flow, realising that none of girls sitting at the window table was taking a blind bit of notice.

"Right, then..." he mumbled and walked off, slightly offended that Ollie's friends weren't interested in his story. Normally, they were always well into his tales of life on the road. He took his disappointment out on the jukebox by giving the temperamental machine a quick kick as he passed, making the record jump even more than it was already doing.

"I just can't believe he'd be so cruel," said Cat sadly.

Sonja, Kerry and Maya collectively shook their heads in astonishment. They'd been all set to quiz Cat (or, actually, get *Sonja* to quiz her) about what had gone on with Ollie at the party, but her news had stumped them.

"I'd never have believed Matt would do something this crappy," Sonja said, staring blankly at the Formica table top in disbelief.

"I mean, I know he's been a real show-off about girls he's been out with," Maya chipped in, her dark brown eyes wide with surprise, "but I didn't think he'd lie like that. Not about something so... so hurtful."

"I know..." Cat nodded mournfully, milking the situation for all it was worth.

"Right," said Sonja, slapping the table surface so hard that the others jumped. "I'm going to confront the creep right now!"

"No!" yelped Cat. The last thing she wanted was to give Matt the chance to deny anything. In fact, she was already wondering if Ollie had done that – he didn't seem to be working in the café today. "No, I think it would be better if we all ignored him from now on. Just blanked him."

"Mmm, maybe you're right, Cat," said Sonja. "He's gone too far this time. I can't believe I was considering easing up on him on Saturday night."

Phew! thought Catrina. *Just as well I came up with that one, then – otherwise they might have all forgiven him by now.*

The tinkle of cutlery caught her attention.

"Anna?" she called over to the young waitress, who was clearing up a neighbouring table. "Is Ollie working today?"

"No," Anna smiled, carrying on loading up her tray. "We swapped days off. He's working tomorrow, with Dorothy or Irene."

"Thanks," said Cat. She needed to catch him soon and try to get this romance going before Matt had a chance to put his side of the story to Ollie. If the damage hadn't been done already. She decided to phone him as soon as she got home.

Breaking away from her thoughts, she realised

that all her friends were staring at her quizzically.

"Well?" said Sonja. "Since you've brought his name up, what exactly did you and Ollie get up to on Saturday? Joe said the two of you were looking *very* cosy before you vanished..."

Cat tipped her head down coquettishly and gave her friends a smug, knowing little smile.

CHAPTER 13

● ●

OLLIE GETS IN DEEPER

Kerry was heading towards the library for her study period before lunch on Tuesday when a strange thing happened. Instead of taking the corridor that led to the library, she found herself walking out through the exit door and hurrying across to the gate that led out on to the road. The road that led to the End.

"Kerry! Boy, am I glad to see you!" Ollie beamed, rubbing his grubby hands on an even grubbier apron.

"Hi, Ol. How've you been?"

What Kerry really wanted to say was "What the hell are you *doing*?" but, unlike Sonja, she wasn't cut out to be confrontational. Skipping a study period was about as bolshy as she got.

"Stressed out, if you must know. I need to talk to you."

And I need to understand what's going on in your head, thought Kerry, agitatedly pushing up her glasses.

"Listen, I'm a bit busy right now, but I'll take a break when I've finished what I'm doing," said Ollie, pointing in the direction of the kitchen. "Can you wait? I'll bring you a cappuccino over."

"Course I will, Ol."

Kerry plonked herself down at the usual table, marvelling that it somehow always seemed to be free. It was as though all the other customers knew instinctively that it was out of bounds – that it was the crowd's table.

Well, whatever crowd we've got left, thought Kerry ruefully.

She glanced over towards the launderette where a little old lady in a pink apron and lime-green hairnet was tap-dancing exuberantly in the doorway. Mad Vera was a great source of amusement to the customers of the café, who often sat and watched her for sheer entertainment value. She did the service washes at the launderette, but seemed to spend most of her time showing off to an invisible audience and having the time of her life.

In a way it must be nice to be like that,

thought Kerry. *No complications, no worries...*

"Earth calling Kerry! Come in, Kerry!"

Kerry snapped out of her daydream to see Ollie laughing at her, his face only inches away from hers.

"Sorry, Ol... I was miles away. Is that for me?" she nodded towards the frothy coffee in front of her.

"Yep, and it's on the house this time. Unless Nick asks, of course. But he's off skiving at the wholesaler's or something, so I wouldn't worry."

Kerry glanced past him at the counter to check Nick hadn't just reappeared – she didn't want Ollie to get into trouble. Dorothy, one of the pensioners who helped out in the daytime, smiled over at her then carried on wiping the work surface.

"I tried to phone you last night," said Kerry.

"Yeah, Mum said. Sorry, I was round at Matt's for a bit and then I didn't really fancy talking to anyone."

"What did Matt have to say for himself?"

"I guess you know all about this rumour business?"

Kerry nodded, cupping her hands round her cappuccino.

"He swears he didn't bad-mouth Cat. And I think I believe him."

"Any particular reason?"

"Well, he's a tactless, thoughtless idiot, but he's not really got it in him to be that evil. And he's really gutted, y'know? He hates the idea that everyone's turning against him."

"What do you think happened then?" asked Kerry, deliberately avoiding bringing up Catrina's name.

"I think the guys that Cat overheard were maybe speaking about someone else and she just picked it up wrong."

"Could be. So..." smiled Kerry awkwardly, wondering who was going to be the first to start talking about the other main event of Saturday's party. "What's stressing you out?"

"Guess."

Kerry knew full well, but just shrugged and smiled instead.

"Kerry, do you think Catrina seriously likes me?"

She looked at him hard, trying to detect what reply he was hoping for. "I'm sure she likes you, Ollie, but I don't think it meant anything, y'know... what happened. How can it, if she was so heartbroken over Matt?"

"Is that what she's told you?" he said, with a look of hope spreading across his face.

"Um, not in so many words," said Kerry, being

economical with the truth. In fact, the previous day Cat had been raving on about how wonderful Ollie was compared to Matt.

"Oh," said Ollie flatly, realising what Kerry wasn't saying. "Trouble is, I think she's really muddled up at the moment. And I was just drunk and did something stupid – I didn't mean to kiss her, I just felt sorry for her, and – and I don't know how it happened really."

"I know," Kerry smiled reassuringly, relieved to hear Ollie's version of events after Cat's sugar-coated side of the story.

"But I'm really worried about hurting her feelings, Kerry," he shrugged. "She's had enough of that recently – and I don't want to hurt her any more!"

"Yeah, but you can't go along with this just 'cause you feel sorry for her!"

"I know," Ollie groaned, rubbing a hand through his mop of hair until it stood up in comical peaks, contrasting incongruously with the woeful look on his face. "But I think I've got to go with it for a bit – she's so vulnerable – and then I'll just try and let her down gently."

"I don't think that's such a good idea, Ol. I mean, what's that going to look like to Matt? If you two have just made up and then he finds out something's going on between you and Cat..."

"I haven't quite figured that out yet," he sighed. "*And* I got a call from Elaine today – she's coming over at the weekend..."

"But she's just a mate, isn't she? That's what you've always said."

"Well, yeah – but in her present state of mind, what d'you think Cat's going to make of it if I tell her?"

"Erm... I think you're just about to get the chance to find out, Ol..."

Ollie looked out of the window to see Catrina beaming at him from the front step.

"Hi, Ollie! Look what I've brought you!" She breezed in and handed Ollie a miniature model of a pale blue Vespa.

"Cat, that's brilliant! Where did you get it?"

"Never you mind, Ollie. It's just my little way of thanking you for... everything."

"Oh, don't be daft, Cat," Ollie smiled awkwardly.

Kerry squirmed in embarrassment.

● ● ●

With her stomach bulging from eating too much spaghetti bolognese followed by Maltesers, Kerry flopped back down on the spare bed in Sonja's room and stared at her poster of Matt Le Blanc that was Blu-tak'd to the ceiling, while her friend sat transfixed by the TV.

"Sonny," she began, desperate to go over the conversation she'd had with Ollie the day before – yet again.

"Hold on, this is just about finished," Sonja shushed her.

Kerry turned her head and watched the last couple of minutes of the programme with her. As the theme music rolled, Sonja pressed the mute button on the remote and gave Kerry her full attention.

"Sorry, I just had to see what was going to happen," she said, plumping up the cushions that lay along the length of her bed. "Now what were you saying?"

"Oh, it's just the Ollie and Cat thing again," said Kerry apologetically. "I just – I just don't get it. I mean, how can anyone go out with someone out of *kind*ness?"

"You tell me," shrugged Sonja. "I've never quite understood what Brad Pitt sees in Jennifer Aniston when he could be having a much better time with me. Some people are just too nice to say no, I guess."

"But only seconds before Cat came in, Ollie was telling me he hoped she *didn't* want to go out with him. And then he's being all sweet with her when she walks in."

"The poor boy's obviously mad, Kez. And too sodding nice for his own good."

"I know," said Kerry, propping herself up on her elbows. "But it's pretty extreme to go out with someone just because you feel a bit guilty!"

"Poor Ollie," muttered Sonja. "Maybe I should tell Cat that he's not really interested..."

"Don't you dare!" Kerry said in alarm. "It would be cruel to her and anyway Ollie—"

"Ollie's a big boy and he's got to sort this one out himself," acknowledged Sonja. "Don't worry, Kez – I'd leave this one up to him."

Kerry relaxed back on to the pillow.

"Son?" she said after a minute's silence between them.

"Uh-huh," Sonja responded, flicking through the TV channels with the sound down.

"D'you think this is going to make things weird for the rest of us? Like, on top of everything else?"

"Things have a habit of sorting themselves out," Sonja answered soothingly, though she wasn't totally convinced herself. "Worrying about it won't help."

Kerry knew Sonja was right, but Kerry was a natural worrier. In fact, she could worry for England.

CHAPTER 14

● ●

MATT'S HOT DATE

Matt couldn't deny it. He was not enjoying the fact that he was in danger of becoming a social outcast.

Since he'd seen Ollie on Monday night he'd heard nothing from anyone, which he took to be a bad sign. Matt didn't feel he had the right to go wading in and call the others – though he'd been on the verge of calling good old Sonja the other night, before bottling out.

He decided it was probably better to stay out of everyone's way till the whole situation blew over. In the mean time, all he could do was hope that Ollie was doing some good PR for him and managing to convince the others of his innocence over the rumour-spreading and his regret over the messy break-up with Cat.

Still, he reminded himself, *at least one good thing's come out of all of this...*

He smiled at the memory of Natasha's phone call an hour earlier, right in the middle of *Top of the Pops.* He'd been feeling down – stuck in on a Friday night with no work on and no friends to see. Even his dad, who'd arrived home the day before, was off out to some posh function up at the golf club, his second home.

Then *she'd* phoned out of the blue, saying that a job had been cancelled and that she was in Winstead for the weekend. And did he fancy going out somewhere, right now? That's the way it had happened, just like that.

Of course it wasn't *just* like that. He'd got her mobile number from Ollie before he'd left on Monday and had called her on Wednesday. Nice and cool; a long enough time after the birthday party and everything so he didn't look *too* desperate. Not that she'd picked up – he'd had to leave some stupid message on her answering service. But it had been worth it. She'd called tonight. They were going on a date. And Matt couldn't wait.

Parking his midnight blue Golf outside The Swan, Matt smoothed his dark hair down and took a deep breath. He really liked this girl. *Really* liked her.

He'd have felt better talking to Ollie again before going out with his sister, but what could he do? It had happened all of a sudden, and anyway, maybe Tasha had already told her brother she was seeing his mate tonight.

That's if Ollie still *was* his mate. Even he'd been ominously quiet all week, despite the fact that they seemed to have straightened everything out on Monday.

Hey, what's done's done, Matt shrugged to himself as he walked up to the side door and rang the doorbell. He'd doused himself in the CKbe his mother had sent him for Christmas, and had put on his best Carharrt top. He had to keep up with what was going on down in London to stand any chance of impressing Tasha.

"Hi!" said Natasha, opening the door.

Matt moved forward to kiss her just as she stepped backwards to grab her keys off the hall table. Awkwardly, he took a step back then headed towards the car and pulled open the passenger door for her.

As she slipped into the seat, Matt admired her shiny helmet of freshly washed, shoulder-length brown hair and caught a glimpse of the brown sheath dress she was wearing under her long leather coat. His heart beat faster. She looked gorgeous. She was utter class. He couldn't blow this.

"Missed me?" he grinned, settling into the driver's seat.

"Erm, hardly, Matt. I've only been gone a couple of weeks," Natasha replied, pulling down the sun visor on her side of the car and checking her make-up in the mirror fixed to the back of it.

Matt felt slightly flummoxed. He wasn't used to girls who didn't just fall for him straight off.

"I thought we could go to Henry's. Do you know it? It's just a little..."

"Henry's?" Natasha laughed. "I haven't been there for years! It used to be packed with tasty guys. Is it still like that?"

Matt furrowed his brow. "I dunno," he said, feeling a bit miffed. She was supposed to be on a night out with him and she was already thinking about other blokes.

He looked at her quizzically. "Haven't been for *years*? How did you get in anyway? You've only just had your seventeenth birthday."

"I guess I've always looked older," sighed Natasha as if she was in the company of a real hick from the sticks. "Don't you ever break the rules, Matt?"

Matt didn't know what to say. Did she want to go to Henry's or didn't she?

And if they did go, would she spend the whole evening with him or would her head be turned by some other 'tasty guy'? Matt didn't relish the idea of competition and thought the whole point of them going out was to spend some time together.

"Is there anywhere else you'd rather go?" he asked, trying to keep the hurt note out of his voice.

"Actually," she said staring out of the window, "I wouldn't have minded going to the End. I haven't been there for ages and it would be fun, just for old times' sake."

"The End?" queried Matt, glancing down at the clock on the dashboard. "Your Uncle Nick'll be locking up there soon. We could always go some other time over the weekend..."

"OK, whatever," Natasha murmured.

"So," said Matt, feeling as if he was on shifting sand, "do you want to go to Henry's or not?"

"Whatever."

What does that mean? Matt worried.

He didn't know what to make of Natasha. She wasn't how he'd imagined at all, but then apart from the snog at the birthday party, and the couple of hours he'd spent with her the following Saturday morning, all he'd known of Natasha up until now was what Ollie had told him – and not all of that was complimentary. According to Ollie, his sister had become pretty big-headed in the year she'd spent in London.

As they sat at the traffic lights, Matt stole another look at her and his heart lurched with excitement again – she was beautiful, with her dark almond eyes and those high cheekbones... He tried to think back to the few times he'd stayed at his dad's during the holidays from boarding school, and wondered why he'd never noticed anyone as special as her.

But then it wasn't surprising really because until he'd finally put his foot down and refused to go any more, he'd spent most of his holidays for the last few years being packed off to his mother and her new family.

As it was, the place he was *supposed* to call home, and the parent who was *supposed* to have custody of him, were both relative unknowns to Matt. It was only once he'd finished school and moved in permanently with his dad that he'd slowly got to know Winstead and the people in it.

"So what's new with you?" Natasha said finally.

"Not much," replied Matt, automatically thinking about how bored and lonely he'd been feeling over the last couple of weeks. "Work's dried up a bit at the moment."

"Your DJing?" asked Natasha. "So what clubs have you played at?"

"Um, none yet," mumbled Matt.

His ambition was to end up on the top dance DJ circuit, playing clubs in London, Ibiza – New York even. But right now, he was struggling to get on to the bottom rung of the ladder.

"Where do you play, then?"

"Well, birthdays, parties... wherever I get a booking."

"What?" snorted Natasha. "Like, 'Here's Whitney Houston's *I Will Always Love You* for Bob and Margaret's fortieth anniversary!'?"

Matt felt himself blush – something he didn't do too often. She was laughing at him.

"Something like that," he muttered.

"Speaking of birthday parties, heard any more about that mad cow you used to go out with?" she asked casually.

"Catrina?" said Matt, momentarily taken aback by hearing her spoken of like that.

But why should I get defensive over Cat? he thought to himself. *She did act as if she was totally demented when she saw me and Tasha together, and—*

Out of nowhere it hit him. That rubbish about him spreading rumours about sleeping with her: it was Cat herself who'd told Ollie about them – it had to be!

Why else would Ollie be all protective and not tell me who he'd heard it from? reasoned Matt.

And what's more – she didn't overhear anything! She's made this whole thing up, just to spite me!

"Little bitch!" he suddenly exclaimed as the truth hit him.

"What?" said Natasha startled at the venom in his voice.

"She's been running telling tales to your brother, that's what she's been doing," snarled Matt.

Natasha stared at him, wondering where this change of character had come from. A second ago he'd sounded like a bit of a buffoon – and one that smelled of too much aftershave – and she'd been regretting her spur-of-the-moment decision to call him. Now he'd suddenly turned into some scary psycho who she really didn't *want* to be with, let alone date.

"What on earth are you talking about?"

"Oh, she told him how I've been boasting about having sex with her," Matt almost spat the words out.

"Really?" said Natasha, alarmed now and completely missing the sarcastic tone in his voice. He was angry with this girl – all because she dared to be hurt about him blabbing about something so private? How could this guy ever have been a mate of her brother's? He was horrible!

"Listen, Matt, I should have said earlier, but

I've got a killer headache and it's getting worse," she improvised. "Could you take me home, please?"

Matt was startled out of his bad temper. His date was over already and it hadn't even begun...

Outside The Swan, Natasha got out of the car without saying a word, slamming the door behind her. Matt knew he'd blown it, but he had no idea why.

● ● ●

Nick had just left the End, happily taking stuffed money bags away to lock up in the small safe he kept in his flat above Nick's Slick Riffs, the record shop next door.

It had been an unusually busy Friday evening and, with a good day's takings under his belt, he was more than happy to let Ollie finish cleaning and locking up. This left him free to go and celebrate with a pint with Bryan (who looked after the record shop for him) down at the Railway Tavern.

"I thought he'd never leave," purred Cat, coming round the counter to where Ollie was stacking the tall milkshake glasses. "In fact, I thought they'd all never leave!"

"Tell me about it!" sighed Ollie, who was tired

111

out after a hard shift and exhausted at the thought of spending quality, romantic time alone with Cat.

He'd managed to avoid it all week, but there was no getting out of it now. She'd been hanging around him all evening as he ran about madly serving everyone, and had happily offered to keep him company when she heard Nick ask his nephew to lock up.

"Well, it's just me and you," she said flirtatiously, reaching around Ollie's waist and undoing his white apron strings.

"Ha ha, I, uh—"

"Shhh."

A dull thunk from above temporarily saved Ollie as Cat dropped her hands and stared at the roof.

"What was that?"

"It'll just be Anna upstairs – she got the bedsit as part of the job here, remember?"

"Hmm," muttered Cat and then grinned her Cheshire Cat grin again. "This is the light switch, isn't it?"

She reached behind Ollie and flicked the switch, plunging them into a semi-darkness that was only broken by the blue fluorescent End-of-the-Line sign in the window, and the soft orange-purple glow of dusky light outside.

Cat moved in closer.

Ollie gulped, seeing no way out. He was glad of the darkness so that Cat wouldn't be able to read the truth in his eyes – that the only feeling he had for her was pity, not lust.

Cat was glad of the lack of light too. It meant that when she kissed Ollie, she wouldn't have to see his funny, familiar face. When she felt his lips on hers, she could imagine it was someone else she was kissing. Maybe even imagine it was Matt...

That was her latest worry. How long she could keep up the pretence of fancying Ollie before she got the chance to snog his face off in front of Matt.

And she couldn't give up until she'd done that – her final revenge.

Ollie was worrying too: worrying about telling Cat that *maybe*, just maybe, she'd been mistaken about what she'd heard at Matt's party.

Worried about how and when to tell Matt that he and Cat were – well, whatever they were.

And worried about how to let Cat know that Elaine was arriving the next day without her taking it all the wrong way.

Just as Ollie felt those arms encircle his waist again, a rapping on the glass door of the café made them both jump.

"Ol! Is that you? Are you still in there?" shouted Nick.

"Yeah! Hold on!" said Ollie, slipping past Cat and running to unlock the front door.

"Hey, Ol, I just had a phone call from that old mate of mine that runs The Bell, remember?"

Ollie looked puzzled. He knew The Bell was the pub off the high street that regularly had bands on, but he didn't know the owner. And Nick had countless numbers of old mates, so many that Ollie could never keep track of them. He nodded anyway.

"He says he booked some band to play next Friday and they've blown him out at short notice. He remembered me telling him about you guys... Would you be up for doing it?"

"Too right!" said Ollie.

It was time The Loud expanded out of the back room of his parents' pub. Even if it was just to the back room at some other pub. At least this one had a proper stage!

"Well, he's coming down to the Railway Tavern in about half an hour. You fancy coming along and talking it over?"

"Absolutely!" Ollie answered excitedly, before suddenly remembering his prior commitment.

He turned and peered at Cat in the gloom of the café behind him.

"Oh, Cat – I really need to meet this guy. I'm really sorry..."

Although sorry was about the last thing Ollie felt.

CHAPTER 15

• •

MAKING UP WITH MATT. OR NOT

"Hey, stranger!"

"Hi, Son," said Matt almost shyly, slipping into the seat across the table from her. "Good to see you again."

Gazing across at her sheepish-looking friend, Sonja couldn't help feeling sorry for him. She'd always really liked Matt, in spite of his cockiness.

She understood Matt because, like him, she was pretty confident and realised that underneath all that bragging and bluster, he was quite a nice bloke. Even quite sensitive, if you looked hard enough.

Right now, she knew he must be feeling pretty down, what with the way everyone had shut him out. Sonja, for her part, was keen to put it all behind them and get their friendship back on track. Especially since Ollie was now convinced that Cat had just misheard the so-called rumour at Matt's party.

"I'm glad you phoned earlier." Sonja smiled warmly at him.

"Me too," he smiled back. "So... am I forgiven yet?"

"Almost," she laughed.

"Did Ollie tell you that I had nothing to do with that rumour about Cat?"

"Uh-huh. He told us earlier in the week."

Matt suddenly wore a hurt puppy dog expression. More like the sort of expression Sonja was used to seeing on Joe's face.

"What, so you knew I was innocent for the last few days and you didn't get in touch with me?"

Unfazed, Sonja grinned at him. "Yeah, well, you deserved to be ignored for a bit. Maybe you had nothing to do with that rumour, but you certainly had plenty to do with making a fool of Cat at Ollie's birthday party."

"So," said Matt quietly, staring down at the table. "Is it just *you* that forgives me?"

"Nah, Kerry and Maya are cool now. So's Joe." Sonja glanced down at her watch. "In fact, they should all be here soon; I told them to come down about eleven."

"What about Catrina?"

"Hey, that might be pushing it a bit, Matt," smiled Sonja ruefully. "Anyway, we haven't seen much of her this week: Ollie's kind of been looking after her..."

Sonja noticed that Matt hadn't reacted to her comment. He obviously didn't know about the burgeoning romance.

Uh-oh, thought Sonja. *And guess who's going to have to tell him...*

"Is Ollie working today? I haven't spoken to him all week," said Matt, glancing through to the kitchen.

I'll bet you haven't, thought Sonja.

"He's due in a bit later, according to Anna," she answered instead.

"Have you heard my news?" Matt asked her, before she could go back to the prickly subject of Catrina and Ollie.

"No," she answered, curious as to what he was going to say.

"I had a date with Natasha last night."

He wasn't looking smug, Sonja noticed. It couldn't have gone very well.

"And?"

"And it lasted for all of ten minutes."

"Matt, babe – you're losing your touch," teased Sonja as the café door tinkled and Maya, Kerry and Joe walked in.

● ● ●

Natasha sat at the kitchen table and agitatedly stirred her black coffee.

She looked up as Ollie came into the kitchen, yawning and rubbing his newly washed hair with a towel.

Irritation made her stir even quicker – she hated to admit defeat and she was just about to have to tell her brother that he had been right. Going out with Matt had been a bad idea.

Ollie had just launched into a chorus of *Wonderwall* as he clattered around the kitchen, fixing himself some breakfast, when Natasha finally said what was on her mind.

"Ol, I need to tell you something."

Damp towel still draped round his neck, Ollie quit his singing and sat down opposite his sister. It had been a long time since they'd had anything like a serious conversation, and as this looked like it might just be the start of one, Ollie wanted to give her his full attention.

"Tasha? What's up?"

"There's something you should know."

"Yeah? Nothing bad, I hope?" Ollie's imagination started going crazy with possibilities.

"I went out with Matt last night."

That was it? Ollie didn't think it was too bad.

He wasn't exactly one hundred per cent comfortable with the idea of his mate dating his sister, but since he'd asked for her mobile number, it wasn't a big surprise.

"So?"

"So, he creeped me out," she shuddered.

"How?"

"Oh, don't worry," she said quickly, seeing the concern in her brother's face, "he didn't do anything. It was just something he said..."

"Well?" The suspense was killing Ollie. "What was he saying exactly?"

"He started going on about sleeping with that Catrina girl."

"What?"

"He was saying something about how she'd caught him boasting about it and how he was mad at her for coming crying to you over it. He's a nasty piece of work, Ollie."

Ollie was livid. So Cat had been right after all...

• • •

Ollie stormed towards the End, mentally ticking off the hours of his shift; how many hours he'd have to hold on to his temper before he'd get the chance to track down Matt and confront him. But, glancing in the bay window as he strode up to the door of the café, Ollie realised it was a matter of seconds rather than hours.

"Ci, you!" he yelled at Matt as he approached the table.

Matt stared up at him blankly while the others froze mid-chat, wondering what was coming next.

"You *were* mouthing off about sleeping with Cat at your party!"

"I wasn't!" protested Matt, completely dumbfounded.

"You bloody were!" barked Ollie. "So stop denying it!"

"For God's sake, Ollie, I told you before—"

"Forget it! First you tell me that Catrina's got it wrong, and now you're saying my sister has too?"

"Tasha?! But I was– I was only trying to tell her that stuff wasn't true!" Matt stammered, trying to get his point across and all too aware of the accusing looks he was getting from all his friends. "And as for Cat—"

"What *about* Cat?" asked Catrina, walking in the café door.

CHAPTER 16

• •

CAT TRIUMPHANT

"I didn't do anything!"

"So, feeling proud of our little self, are we?" Sonja sneered at Matt, her arms folded on the table in front of her.

Being the closest to Matt, she felt particularly betrayed and disappointed in him. She'd defended him, got the others together today to rally around him again, and now she felt let down.

"Don't be daft, Son – you know I didn't—"

Matt stopped before he got to the end of his sentence. He didn't like the look on Sonja's face one little bit.

"How could you do it, Matt? I thought we were all supposed to be friends?" said Maya, her tone curt and serious.

"Bragging about your 'conquest' – how could you lie about something like that?" Kerry burst out, looking close to tears.

Matt swung his gaze round to Joe and looked at him pleadingly. He was shocked by the stony expression on Joe's face. Were they all against him now? Just when he'd thought it was all sorted?

"Please! I—"

"Don't bother, Matt," snapped Sonja. "We've given you enough chances. *And* you've never *once* apologised to poor Cat!"

Still sitting rigid with shock, Matt turned to stare at 'poor Cat', who'd been tearfully clinging on to Ollie since she'd walked in and found out what all the commotion was about.

Meeting his gaze, she knew it was her chance.

"See what he's like? He's just a liar!" she said to her friends, before looking up adoringly at Ollie. "Thank God I'm with you now!"

Everyone, including Matt, stared openmouthed as Catrina ran her hand round the back of Ollie's head and pulled his mouth on to hers.

"Well, cheers, everyone! Thanks for the support, you know? And thanks for the floor show, Catrina!" barked Matt, grabbing his jacket and storming out of the café.

Hearing the bell above the door jangle

violently, Cat broke away from Ollie, trying very hard to stifle the grin that was threatening to break out on her face.

At last! she thought. *Now Matt knows exactly how it feels to be humiliated in public. And it happened without me even trying!*

Struggling to settle her features into an expression of hurt, rather than one of triumph, she turned to the others.

"Listen... Don't worry about me..."

"Oh, Cat, don't worry, we won't have anything more to do with him. He doesn't deserve to have any friends after this," said Maya grimly.

"Thanks. Thanks, you guys," Cat said humbly. "Anyway, I'd better go... I'd like to be on my own now."

"Cat, try not to let this get to you, OK? He's just not worth it," said Ollie, concerned that she was just going to go home and cry.

The fact was, the strain of having to pretend to be the injured party was almost too much for Catrina. She'd finally got what she wanted, but she knew she'd have to wait until she was on her own before she could relish the feeling properly. Far from going home to cry, all she wanted to do was jump around her room for joy.

I've won! she sang in her head. *I got revenge!*

Making one final effort to look upset, she kissed her finger then stretched over and pressed it to Ollie's lips. "I'll be fine, Ollie. Honest."

It was only then that she realised how quiet the busy café had become. Every customer at every table had swivelled around to witness the scene. And Cat kind of liked that.

CHAPTER 17

● ●

REGRETS AND SOLUTIONS

Thankful that her mother was out, Cat had spent some time blasting out her favourite CDs, dancing round the flat and singing at the top of her voice. She'd given in to gloating and was revelling in the distinctly pleasurable feeling of knowing that Matt had finally got what he deserved.

Until she flopped down breathless and exhausted on the sofa. Until she realised, to her dismay, that she felt strangely empty.

What's bugging me? she asked herself, running through the events of the last couple of weeks in her head.

One part of it was obvious: her guilt over using Ollie was getting in the way of enjoying her victory.

God! How am I going to sort that out? she

worried, aware that now her plan of action had succeeded, she wanted out of this messy, lovey-dovey business with Ollie as quickly as possible.

Pity I don't fancy him really. It would make everything a lot easier...

She turned over on her side and sighed. It was all so hugely frustrating. Every bloke she'd ever been out with up until now had been a total loser and ended up hurting her. Now here she was, with the potential to go out with the nicest guy in the world, and she knew her chances of caring for him *that* way were zilch.

Why do I always fall for the bad boys? And when am I going to meet someone who's as good to me as Ollie, someone who I actually want to fall in love with...?

But something else was bugging her, something that she hardly wanted to admit to herself...

She missed Matt. She missed Matt so much it hurt.

● ● ●

Shivering, Cat fastened the buttons on her jacket against the afternoon breeze that had sprung up. She was hurrying past the part of the park where the kids' playground was, but the giggling and laughter coming from there didn't cheer her up as it normally did.

Heading back towards the End, Cat's head was in a swirl. She still didn't know how she was going to break it off with Ollie yet – she wanted to do it in such a way that she kept face (Cat wasn't about to forget who came first in her world), but she didn't want to jeopardise her friendship with Ollie either.

I'll think of something, she shivered again. *I always do.*

After her earlier bout of guilt, the one thing Cat *was* sure of was that she wanted all this madness to stop and to get back to normal. All this scheming and plotting was exhausting. She was even starting to forget who she'd told which lie to. And she couldn't bear torturing Matt any more.

Matt, you idiot, she thought to herself, *you deserved everything you got. But...*

As selfish as she could be, Catrina wasn't completely heartless. She knew Matt was having a miserable time of it. She'd caught sight of him one day during the week at the wheel of his car, waiting at a red light, and the gloom on his face was almost heart-breaking.

She'd momentarily felt truly sorry for him and the feeling had surprised her. Had she caused that? Was it because of her that he was so unhappy?

And now, after what had happened in the café earlier, he must *seriously* be down. Matt loved the crowd and now none of them was speaking to him. Thanks to Catrina and whatever fluke conversation Natasha had had with him.

The problem with Cat's revenge plan was that she hadn't thought long-term. And now the prospect of Matt's punishment being permanent didn't fill her with any joy. She realised that she didn't want him excluded from the gang for ever.

Aside from the time they'd gone out together – she shivered again as she remembered kissing him – Cat missed the way things had been even before they'd dated, when they used to tease each other and banter constantly. Now everything felt flat and boring.

Matt was one of those charismatic types who always kept everyone entertained; excitement seemed to follow him around and life felt distinctly dull without him, especially now Catrina had run out of steam on her revenge plot.

Coming out of the park, Cat crossed through the traffic and followed the road round until she was standing across from the End.

Come on, girl! she told herself as she stepped off the pavement and walked towards the café. *You can do this.*

Pushing the door open, she caught sight of

Ollie sitting on a high stool by the counter, holding hands with a hippyish girl on the stool next to him.

Here we go! she thought as Ollie turned and spotted her, shock written across his face. *Fate's just done me its second favour of the day!*

"Ollie! How could you!" sobbed Cat, running back out into the street as Ollie and Elaine stared after her.

CHAPTER 18

• •

MAKING UP IS HARD TO DO

"Cat!" said Ollie as Cat opened the front door to his urgent knocking and ringing.

Cat swore under her breath. Because he was still on his shift, she hadn't expected Ollie to follow her back round to the flat so soon, and hadn't quite had time to prepare her lines.

Better just wing it, she told herself. *It's worked up till now.*

"I'm so sorry!" said Ollie breathlessly. "I meant to tell you Elaine was coming over this weekend, but I—"

"It's OK," Cat managed a brave smile and ushered him into the hallway. "Come on in."

"She's just my friend, that's all – it's not some big romance like all you girls think!" Ollie continued to protest.

Cat pulled a tissue out of a box on the kitchen worktop and dabbed her dry eyes.

"I think– I think it's more than that, Ollie."

"No, honestly—"

"Wait, Ollie, listen to me," Cat said, placing her fingers gently over his lips. "I'm not angry – really I'm not. It's just that I can see more than you can at the moment, and you like Elaine a lot more than you're admitting to yourself."

"But I—" he tried to mumble through Cat's fingers.

"No, please don't. I know I'm right," Cat smiled sorrowfully.

"Bu—"

"And, Ollie, I think you two are *so* right for each other; better than we could ever be," she continued dramatically. "In fact, I think we work better just as friends..."

Cat noticed Ollie didn't try to contradict her. She also noticed the expression in his eyes, which looked a little like relief.

God, does he want out of this as badly as I do? she wondered fleetingly to herself.

"Are you sure, Cat?" he asked finally, clasping her fingers with his own.

"Oh, yes," she nodded with a sniffle or two, just to keep up appearances. "Actually, Ollie, I'd like us all to be friends again... Matt too."

"What, after everything he's done to you?"

"Yes, even after everything he's done. I– I forgive him."

"Are you sure?" asked Ollie, stunned at how magnanimous Cat was being.

"Yes. I just want everything to be back the way it was," said Cat with – for once in this conversation – genuine feeling. She knew that she and Matt could never be a couple again after all that had happened, but if she could just be *close* to him, as a friend... "Do you think that could happen, Ollie?"

"Don't worry, Cat, I'll sort it out! If you can forgive him, I reckon we all can!"

"Thank you, Ollie!" she beamed. "Now, you get back to that girl of yours!"

"Honestly, she's not—" Ollie began to protest then stopped himself. Instead, he planted a quick kiss on Cat's cheek before heading out of the flat.

"Cat – you're a star!" he shouted up the stairwell as he jumped the steps two at a time.

Just as he vanished round the bend, Cat took a little bow to her imaginary audience.

● ● ●

The three girls stood in the doorway of the café and stared at the scene before them.

"Sonny, Kerry, Maya, c'mere! I was just telling the guys this joke about a lobster going into a bar. Heard it yet?"

"Er, no..." said Sonja. Kerry and Maya swapped puzzled glances. Out of habit, they walked over to the window table where the 'guys' – Joe, Elaine and, surprisingly, Matt – budged up to make room for them.

Completely ignoring the girls' discomfort – Kerry, Sonja and Maya were, after all, strictly not on speaking terms with Matt – Ollie proceeded to tell the joke, laughing uproariously at the punchline.

"Like all your jokes, that was rubbish, Ol," Matt said amiably, getting to his feet. "Er, sorry to make you move again, people, but I said I'd give Elaine a lift to the bus station."

Elaine stood up, the various bangles round her wrist jangling as she picked up her embroidered rucksack from the floor.

"Can't afford the train," she shrugged, smiling at the new arrivals. "Sorry I didn't catch you lot this time round – it was just a flying visit. Felt I had to make up for missing this one's birthday."

Laughing, she reached over and ruffled Ollie's hair.

Sonja felt Kerry stiffen beside her; no doubt she'd be worrying about what exactly that affectionate gesture meant.

"Thanks for taking her, Matt. My Sunday shift starts in..." Ollie glanced at his watch, "...ten minutes, so it would have been a bit of a mad rush."

"No problem," grinned Matt, shuffling his way out of the booth.

"See you soon, gorgeous," said Elaine, bending over to give Ollie a peck on the lips.

"I'll phone you during the week, E," Ollie smiled up at her. "Safe journey."

Sonja could feel prickles of curiosity practically fly from Kerry's body.

"What are you lads playing at?" Sonja asked Ollie and Joe as soon as the door had clanged shut. "What's with the big buddy act?"

"Listen, I got a few things sorted out with Cat yesterday," Ollie began to explain.

"Like?" asked Sonja tetchily.

"Like, we're not an item."

Sonja felt Kerry shudder slightly.

Well, at least that'll be one thing less for her to worry about, thought Sonja.

"And she's decided that life's too short to hold grudges. So she wants us all to make up with Matt," he shrugged. "And I guess if she's willing to forgive him, then we all can."

He looked at them each in turn, beaming one of his biggest smiles. Ollie hated conflict and he'd felt so much better since he'd made peace with Matt the night before.

Not that Matt had made it easy.

"But she made that whole rumour thing up!" he'd moaned. "Why should I forgive her?"

"I'm sure she *didn't* start that rumour – it's all some misunderstanding. Anyway, you started all this by being a tactless git, so let's call it quits," Ollie had reasoned.

Eventually, Matt had come round to the idea, since it meant being back with his mates, and had agreed to meet Ollie and Joe on Sunday as a first step towards coming back into the fold. And it was agreed that he'd leave Ollie to smooth the ways with the girls.

"Well, I'm sorry, but I just think it's all a bit too easy," sniffed Sonja. "Take it from me, my cousin wouldn't just forgive Matt after what he did. Not her."

"Sonny, I know it's hard to get your head round this one, but Catrina's quite capable of being kind, you know," insisted Ollie. "She's no saint, but she told me she felt really uncomfortable about Matt being out of the gang, so she decided it was up to her to do something about it."

Up until this point, Sonja had had every sympathy with Cat over the whole episode. But now something didn't quite add up. This wasn't a side of Catrina that she knew.

In all the years they'd grown up and hung around together, Cat had always been an attention-seeking drama queen, and this new, kindly, forgiving, martyr act didn't ring entirely true. Was it possible that her cousin had learned a few lessons and changed for the better? Sonja doubted it.

"Come on, Sonja – don't be so mean," said Maya. "I think it's brilliant if Catrina's thinking like this, and if Matt's happy with that, then who are we to criticise?"

"But Matt was really out of order—" Kerry began, still upset at Matt's behaviour.

"But Matt made a mistake, right? I mean, Sonja, what about that time you had a fringe cut that made you look like a complete spanner? And Kerry, I distinctly remember you buying a highly dodgy Aerosmith CD not so very long ago, however well you thought you'd hidden it from us..."

The stupidity of his argument made everyone start to snigger – exactly as Ollie had hoped.

"And we've got to get this sorted 'cause poor old Elaine came all the way here to visit me and all she heard was me mouthing off about all our troubles," Ollie continued. "I want us all to be back to normal next time I see her or she'll never want to see me again!"

"And, um, when is that?" asked Kerry in a little high-pitched voice. "The next time you'll see her, I mean?"

Kerry, you're so transparent! Sonja laughed to herself. *Ollie must be able to see that you're fishing for information a mile away!*

She gazed out of the window for a second while the others babbled away around her. Sonja was glad, she had to admit to herself, that things might be getting back to normal for the crowd.

And maybe Cat has changed into a calm, rational human being, she thought, trying to be more generous about her cousin. *It's a crazy world, so you never know...*

As if on cue, Sonja spotted Mad Vera outside the launderette opposite, attempting to do the Macarena with a passing businessman who was desperately trying to shake her off.

Yep, thought Sonja, grinning in spite of herself, it's a crazy world.

CHAPTER 19

• •

FANCY MEETING YOU

Cat's heart skipped a beat.

It was Sunday night and she was on her way round to The Swan where Ollie had organised a get-together in the back room of the pub. He'd phoned her earlier to say everyone was fine, everyone – including Matt – was happy to start over, and that he wanted them all to come round to his that evening for a bit of a celebration.

Catrina had looked out her favourite sundress and a cute little cardi to match – she wanted to look her best for her first peace-time meeting with Matt.

But that first meeting was happening quicker than she thought.

"Matt! Wait!" she called. He stopped walking, turned and looked slightly shaken to see her.

"What, no car? I'm not used to seeing you use your legs!" she said as brightly as she could, once she caught up with him.

Matt flailed around for an answer; he hadn't anticipated bumping into her so early either.

"So, did your fancy car break down then?"

He looked at her warily, unsure if this was old-time friendly teasing or the start of some barbed and bitter barrage.

"No, I just thought I might have a beer tonight, so I left it at home," he answered flatly.

"Ooh, you're so grown-up and responsible," simpered Cat then realised how sarcastic it probably sounded.

"Hey, Cat, I thought the whole point of tonight was to reach a truce?" said Matt with an edge of irritation to his voice.

Catrina felt flustered; she didn't want him to get the wrong idea. She *was* going to try her best to be civil because she *did* miss his friendship. And him. Not that she was going to admit that out loud to anybody.

"Of course, it is!" she smiled sweetly at him, linking her arm into his and leading Matt along the road towards The Swan. "Now, let's go in together and show the others how civilised we can be!"

Being so close to him, Cat caught a whiff of

the aftershave he wore – and felt her heart skip a
beat again.

• • •

"Here's to us!" said Ollie, holding up a glass of
orange juice.

Matt was the only one in the back room of The
Swan with anything remotely alcoholic in front of
him: Ollie's parents – with the exception of his
birthday party when they bent the rules a little –
were hot on keeping strictly to age limits when it
came to serving drinks.

"Pity Maya couldn't be here," sighed Kerry
who was all aglow at having her friends back
together.

"Well, you know what she's like: she never
seems to want to come out on a night before
school," shrugged Sonja. Sometimes sensible old
Maya's lack of spontaneity could put a real
damper on things. But not tonight.

The atmosphere had thawed out much quicker
than Ollie could have hoped for – helped, of
course, by the fact that Catrina and Matt had
arrived together and seemed relatively at ease with
each other.

Ollie was pleased. Now that their friendship
seemed back on the right track, and now that his

stupid romantic entanglement with Cat was over, he could get seriously excited about the gig that was coming up.

"So, are you all coming to see us on Friday then?"

"Of course!" said Cat and Sonja in unison. One thing the cousins had in common was their love of a good night out.

"Show them the poster for the gig, Joe!" Ollie nudged his friend. "Joe went and picked this up from the bloke at The Bell. He's putting them all around town!"

Joe pulled the rolled-up poster out of his inside jacket pocket and spread it out across the table for the gang to read.

"But it's just someone else's poster with your band's name slapped on top!" said Cat, picking at the sticky white label with 'The Loud' written on it in black marker pen.

"Well, they cancelled at the last minute – the owner couldn't afford to go printing a load of new posters!"

"Hey, Ol – it says here it'll be 'a night of old favourites'. What does that mean?" asked Matt. "Aren't you playing your own stuff?"

"Nah – the other band were just going to be doing covers of other people's songs, so we'll have to do the same," explained Ollie, slightly disappointed by his friends' lack of enthusiasm. "Anyway, that's how we got this gig – Nick told the bloke at The Bell how good we were at doing old songs at my party."

"Um, Ol," said Sonja, pointing at the poster. "What does this bit mean – 'plus extremely special VIP guest'?"

"Dunno," said Ollie, scratching his head and reading the line over. "Must be a publicity stunt the last band were going to do."

"But Ollie, *your* band's name's on this poster now," Sonja tried to spell it out to him. "People who buy tickets are – strangely enough – going to expect to see an 'extremely special VIP guest'!"

Ollie scratched his head again and looked at Joe, who just shrugged his shoulders.

"I hadn't thought of that!"

"Well, you'd better think of something fast or everyone's going to be demanding their money back by the end of the night!" said Sonja.

"Your dad used to play in local mod bands back in the '60s, didn't he? You could always get him in on bongos or something!" Cat giggled.

"Oh yeah, Cat – like I'd really let my dad ruin our set. Actually, knowing him, he'd probably steal the show..."

"So if your special guest's not super-mod Stuart Stanton, let me see..." said Cat, drumming her fingers in the table. "Can the lucky punters of Winstead expect to see someone like Richard Ashcroft from the Verve? No? Jay Kay from Jamiroquai? Erm, Kate Moss? Liam Gallagher? Robbie Williams?"

Ollie'd been grinning while she ran through her list of stars, but as she reached the end of her wish-list of celebs, his face fell.

"They won't *really* be expecting anyone famous to turn up, will they?" he winced.

"Better get that black marker out again," remarked Matt with a cheeky smile.

"How come?" asked Ollie.

"You're going to have to run round town crossing that bit out on all the posters."

Ollie dropped his head in his hands and groaned.

It was only when he felt a wet kiss land on his forehead that he sprang to life again: looking up, he saw Cat's face loom in front of him as she stretched across the table.

"There, there," she purred, brushing his hair away from his face affectionately. "It'll be all right..."

Ollie felt panic rise in his chest. Not only did he have to worry about this stupid special guest business, but now Cat was getting all gooey on him again.

And why did she gave him that conspiratorial wink as she slid back down into her seat? It didn't help. It didn't help at all.

CHAPTER 20

● ●

A VERY IMPORTANT PERSON

The telephone had been ringing for ages.

"Ollie!" shouted Anna, her hands full with a tray of dirty dishes – it had been really busy for a Tuesday lunchtime. "*Ollie!!*"

Crashing the tray down on the counter, Anna leapt over and grabbed the phone from the wall.

"Hello?"

"Could I speak to someone called Ollie, please?"

Anna glanced round the café. "I wish you could, but I don't know where he is right this second."

"Well, maybe you can help. My name's George Callaghan – I'm a reporter here at the *Winstead Gazette*. I'm ringing to see if you can confirm a rumour we've heard..."

"What rumour?" she asked, stepping back and peering into the kitchen to see if she could locate the missing Ollie.

"According to my sources, a top pop star will be guesting on stage with some local band called The Lout this Friday at The Bell. Is there any truth in the rumour?"

Anna laughed. "The Lout? Actually, it's The Loud. And no, I don't think the rumour's true."

"I was given the name of 'Ollie' as my contact. Does he work there?"

"He's supposed to, but, as I say, he's not here right now..."

The reporter sighed with frustration and left his name and number for Ollie to call back.

"We'd be more than happy to send a photographer down. Please ask him to phone me."

"Sure," said Anna then turned to see Ollie bustle through from the kitchen.

"Where did you vanish to?"

"Sorry – just popped out the back for a minute. Cat had, er, something to show me."

Anna raised an eyebrow. "Well, while you were looking at, um, whatever your friend had to show you, some reporter from the *Winstead Gazette* rang you – wanting to know which pop star was going to turn up at your gig on Friday."

"So, Sonja was right!" Ollie groaned.

"What do you mean?" asked Anna, picking up her tray again and barging past Ollie through to the kitchen.

"That stupid poster," he said, following her. "It says we have a special guest and Sonja said people would take it seriously."

"Doh!" teased Anna, crashing dirty plates into the sink.

"It's not funny, Anna," Ollie sighed. "I don't fancy being bottled off the stage by people who are expecting some mega-star to turn up!"

"So? What are you going to do?" asked Anna more seriously. "Are you going to make an announcement at the start of the gig or something?"

"Uh, no..." he muttered, crossing his arms and scuffing at the floor tiles with the toe of his trainer. "We've got a kind of contingency plan."

Anna noticed his downcast expression. It couldn't be a very good plan for him to look *that* miserable.

"Hey, Ollie, it can't be that bad!" she tried to jolly him along. "You look like someone's just stolen your Vespa. Are you OK?"

"Yeah, yeah – don't worry," he said, not sounding particularly convinced by his own assurances. "It's all under control."

• • •

Kerry was a mess of nerves by Friday evening. There were four problems battling for worry time in her head.

First, the *Winstead Gazette* had run a feature the day before about some mystery pop star turning up at The Loud's gig, which obviously wasn't going to happen.

Added to that, not only had Ollie been weird and evasive all week, but also no one had heard from Cat since Sunday night, apart from Maya having caught sight of her at school.

If that wasn't enough, there was the tummy-tingling fact that Kerry was about to see Mick, the guitarist from The Loud, for the first time since Matt's party. And Sonja was adamant that something could happen between Kerry and him that night.

"What're you doing, Kerry?"

Lewis was standing in the doorway, a slobbering Barney in tow as usual, and a serious expression on his face. Lewis loved watching Kerry getting ready to go out. But he always had to ask questions.

"Just putting on my make-up, Lewis. I'm trying to look pretty."

Lewis shut one eye, looked her up and down,

then delivered his considered verdict. "You look pretty all the time."

Then, obviously embarrassed at paying her a compliment, he turned and ran down the stairs making a loud crashing aeroplane sound.

Bless the little monster, smiled Kerry to herself. Her little brother always said the right thing, even if Kerry never quite believed it herself.

The fact that Lewis also thought the Teletubbies and Cilla Black were pretty was irrelevant; his unquestioning confidence in her always had a positive effect.

Will Mick think I look pretty? Will anyone? she wondered pulling on her sparkly blue shirt again to be on the safe side. It seemed to be a bit of a winner and she needed all the help she could get to calm her nerves.

"KERRYKERRYKERRY! Sonja's HERE!" Lewis yelled up the stairs.

As the two girls headed off, Kerry couldn't help feeling inferior once she spotted how effortlessly great Sonja looked. Even in combats, a spaghetti strap vest and trainers, she did not disappoint.

"You look nice, Sonny. As usual."

"So do you, Kez. And I'm sure Mick will agree with me."

"Well, maybe..." said Kerry uncertainly.

"Aw! Come on, Kerry, I'll take a bet on him chatting you up tonight!"

Kerry squirmed, half out of embarrassment and half out of excitement. She decided to get Sonja safely off the subject of her love-life and talk to her about some of the other stuff that was rattling about in her brain.

"So, Son – I've been thinking about the way Cat kissed Ollie on Sunday—"

"Oh, not again!" sighed Sonja. "I told you before, it wasn't any big deal! She was joking about, trying to cheer him up about the VIP thing on the poster."

"But after the two of them almost going out together, and she's gone AWOL all week, and Ollie's been kind of secretive..."

"You're reading too much into it, Kez," Sonja comforted her friend. "I mean Ollie was sitting there with a big lipstick print on his forehead looking about as pleased as your little brother does when his *granny* tries to kiss him. It wasn't the look of a boy in love!"

Kerry shrugged and stared at the cars whizzing past them. Sonja was right. But still...

"And Ollie's just stressed out and busy rehearsing for his big night. Joe's the same! And you're not trying to suggest anything's going on between *Joe* and Cat, are you?"

Kerry giggled at the thought of shy-boy Joe and mouthy Cat together. Joe wouldn't last a minute.

"But what about this stuff in the paper?" said Kerry, getting serious again, and pushing her glasses up in that nervous way she had. "What's Ollie going to do about everyone thinking there's a celebrity turning up?"

"Ollie'll sort it out – he's a big boy!" said Sonja, grabbing her friend by the arm and getting ready to cross the road as soon as there was a break in the traffic. "Now listen – stop worrying! We're going to have a good time tonight, OK?"

"I hope so," muttered Kerry, feeling the butterflies in her tummy start fluttering around in earnest.

• • •

The Loud had played a few numbers to the packed crowd in The Bell and had received a politely enthusiastic response.

It's going to be all right, Ollie assured himself, although when he'd seen how many people had turned up, his heart had sunk at first, knowing that only the publicity from the paper had made the ticket sales zoom up in the last couple of days.

They like us. It's going to be OK...

But two more songs in and Ollie began to be aware of a certain restlessness in the audience. There was a lot of shuffling going on and plenty of talking and muttering too.

"Hey, where's this special guest, then!" Ollie heard someone bellow as one number came to an end.

He turned round to Joe and nodded.

"Now!" he mouthed, and Joe turned to the wings and gave someone a quick thumbs-up.

"OK, ladies and gentlemen," Ollie yelled into the mike. "You've all been waiting for her and here she is – our very special guest, the one and only... Catwoman!"

Uncertain of what was coming but suitably intrigued, the crowd gave a cheer – which was practically drowned out by the sound of a revving engine.

A gasp of excitement spread round the venue as Ollie's Vespa entered stage left, with a leopard-skin, cat-suited girl astride it, complete with mask and tail. To ear-splittingly loud cheers and whistling, she did a quick circuit of the stage as the band struck up the introduction to *Batman*, done Prince-style.

"Thanks for this, Cat," Ollie whispered as she leapt off the bike and handed it to him.

"My pleasure," Cat winked before twirling back to her audience.

From her long, painted talons to her kitten heel boots, Cat was perfect as a one-woman show-stealer. But Ollie didn't mind; through the theme tune, plus the other *Batman* classic, *Hold Me, Thrill Me, Kiss Me, Kill Me*, it was all he could do to sing the words without laughing. The show had turned into pure kitsch and the crowd were loving it.

By the finale – a rendition of Tom Jones' corny *What's New Pussycat?* – the whole audience were yelling along to the words as Cat egged them on by dancing at the edge of the stage and twirling her tail seductively. For once in her life, OTT was exactly the right mode.

"They love us!" Ollie shouted to the rest of the band in surprise above the deafening applause at the end of the set.

"They love Tiddles, you mean!" Rob shouted back, nodding at Catrina.

But it doesn't matter, Ollie grinned, looking back out at the sea of laughing faces and watching Cat curtseying cutely. *As long as we weren't bottled off...*

"Enjoy yourself then, Miss Kitty?" said Ollie, flinging his arm around Catwoman's shoulders as the cheering continued.

"You bet!" beamed Cat, blowing kisses to the boys baying for her attention.

Of all her recent award-winning performances, this, she decided, had definitely been the most fun.

CHAPTER 21

● ●

THANK YOU AND GOOD NIGHT

Exhausted and elated, everyone piled back to the End after the gig.

In anticipation of The Loud's triumph, Nick – who'd been on duty in the wings at The Bell, helping Cat find the ignition switch before she roared on stage – had managed to get a special extension to the café's licence to stay open until 1.00 am.

The place was packed. Apart from people the members of The Loud genuinely knew, Nick was happily letting in anyone who showed him a ticket from the gig.

As everyone swarmed into the small café, Ollie, helped by Anna, cleared the freestanding tables from the middle of the room and stashed them in the kitchen, creating a minute dance floor.

The jukebox had been rammed full of coins and music was belting out. Already bodies were swaying to the song that was playing – mostly boys' bodies, and all because Cat, still resplendent in her Catwoman costume, was dancing, arms aloft, in the middle of them all.

"Pity you didn't catch the gig," Ollie smiled at Anna as they both rested for a second from their efforts, leaning on either side of the doorway that lead from the kitchen, and surveyed the scene before them.

"But I did," grinned Anna, giving him a sideways look.

"Did you?" asked Ollie in surprise.

He liked Anna a lot, from what little he knew of her, but she seemed to keep her private life so much to herself that it hadn't occurred to him to invite her. In fact the only reason he thought she was here now, he realised guiltily, was because Nick had asked her to work.

"Yes," nodded Anna. "I watched from the back. It was a big success, wasn't it?"

"Well, yeah," Ollie replied. "I mean, I really want us to get out and play our own music, but tonight was fun. Thanks to *her*."

Anna looked over in the direction of Ollie's gaze to where Catrina was dancing, her Cheshire Cat grin visible despite the mask she was still wearing.

"Where did she get the costume from?" asked Anna.

"She made it," Ollie answered. "That was her idea, along with being our VIP guest."

"Was that what she was showing you the other day when I took that call for you?"

Ollie nodded. "I just wanted to keep quiet about the whole thing, in case it all went horribly wrong."

"Well, it didn't. And look – your star wants you," Anna said, pointing over to Cat, who was waving frantically at Ollie. "Better hurry over – you owe her!"

"Yeah, you're right," grinned Ollie as he made his way round the counter and over to the beckoning Cat.

• • •

Kerry, Sonja and Maya pushed their way through the dancers and stood on the edge of the makeshift dance floor, totally gobsmacked.

"I think I've died and gone to heaven," sighed Sonja.

"All these cute boys in a tiny, confined space. It's just too much for a girl to take," grinned Kerry.

"Wall-to-wall totty," giggled Sonja.

"Yes, but they're probably all idiots, judging by

the way they're drooling over Catwoman," sniffed Maya.

"Thanks for bringing us back down to earth, Mrs Sensible," Sonja grumbled to her friend. "Don't you ever fancy anyone? C'mon, you must do!"

Sonja brought her face right up close to Maya's, making it clear that she wouldn't accept an evasive answer. Kerry did the same. The two girls started giggling at Maya's obvious embarrassment.

"Tell us! Tell us! Tell us!" they chanted.

"Boys aren't a priority to me!" she said, looking slightly irate.

"Aw, Miss Prim," teased Sonja, "you're kidding us!"

Maya's dark eyes flashed and Kerry suddenly felt mean.

"OK, OK, if you must know, I've fancied quite a few people, but my parents would freak out if I actually went out with anyone," Maya admitted. "It just wouldn't be worth the grief."

"But why would they freak?" asked Sonja, finding Maya's situation hard to comprehend. Her own family were so laid-back they never batted an eyelid at anything their children said or did.

"They want me to concentrate on my studies. So that's what I'm going to do. Happy now?"

Keen to take the pressure off Maya – and aware that Sonja would keep going with this interrogation unless she was diverted – Kerry cocked her head in the direction of Joe, who was standing up at the far end of the café.

"I wonder who Joe fancies?" she mused. "You never see him with a girl, do you?"

Teasingly Sonja said, "Why, Kerry? Don't tell us *you* fancy him?!"

"No, of course not. But he must fancy someone. Everyone fancies someone…"

Just as she spoke, Kerry spotted a face – and a hairstyle – she couldn't miss.

"Hi, Kerry! Hi, Maya – Sonja!" said Elaine, grinning broadly. "Glad I found you – I didn't spot you at the gig!"

"Hi! We didn't see you either," Kerry responded, smiling at both Elaine and the shaven-headed young guy beside her. "Ollie didn't say you were coming tonight!"

"I didn't think I'd be able to till Jakey here offered to drive me down."

Kerry smiled again at the bald boy whose only facial hair consisted of his eyebrows – pierced, she noticed – and an arty little goatee. She felt a dig in her back: Sonja must be thinking the same thing. Maybe Ollie and Elaine *were* only mates, and maybe Jakey here was Elaine's love interest.

"Have you seen Ollie?" Elaine asked. "I haven't caught up with him yet."

"He's over there – dancing with the leopard lady!" said Kerry, pointing to the crammed dance area behind Elaine.

At the same time, she saw two grinning figures ambling over in their direction: Mick and Rob.

Could Sonja be right? Kerry thought to herself, her heart beating faster than the drum beat on the hip-hop track blasting from the jukebox.

• • •

From his vantage point over by the counter, Joe watched as Rob and Mick began chatting to the girls and saw the way Kerry's face lit up as she gazed at Mick.

Frustration raged within him and, for a fleeting second, Joe felt like punching the wall behind him. Up until now he'd had a great night; the response from the crowd, the pats on the back and words of praise he'd had from friends and strangers alike had filled him with a new sense of confidence.

In fact, he'd felt so confident, he'd decided that tonight was the night to go over and talk to Kerry properly; maybe even ask her out, if things went well.

But now he'd lost his chance. It looked as if Mick was about to sweep her off her feet – so what was the point of trying now? He'd only make a fool of himself and lose the friendship of one of the few girls he got on with. He felt utterly depressed.

Home time, he sighed to himself and pushed his way through the crush towards the café door.

Feeling the chill night air on his face, Joe practically tripped over Matt, who was hunched up on the front step.

"All right?" asked Joe, hovering over his friend, hands stuffed in his jacket pockets.

"Nah, not really," Matt replied, shaking his head. "And you? Why are you off?"

Joe shrugged. "Bored, I guess."

The two lads, neither of them in the mood to talk, stayed companionably quiet for a few seconds.

"Well, I'm off – 'night," said Joe finally, before loping off along the street.

"Yeah, 'night, Joe," Matt muttered after him.

Matt was lost in thought. Since he'd watched the show – watched Cat, that is – he just couldn't stop thinking about her.

Yeah, so she's vain, he told himself, *but so's Tasha and you'd never see her risk embarrassing herself, getting up there and giving it a go.*

And succeeding – brilliantly, he'd had to admit.

And sure, Cat can be a pain, he reminded himself, *but at least she's fun, at least she's always up for a laugh.*

Matt's mind flashed back to the night at Ollie's party and wondered what on earth he'd seen in the beautiful but boring Natasha. Compared to Cat's larger-than-life personality, Tasha seemed as exciting as a cardboard cut-out.

There was an uncomfortable feeling in his chest. It was a new feeling for him and it took him a while, sitting on the cold front step, to work out what it was: regret.

The bell clanged behind him as the door was pulled open and the sound of the partying suddenly increased in volume.

"Oh... Matt."

Catrina, now maskless and with her blonde curls bouncing round her face, was surprised to find him there.

Matt, equally startled, jumped to his feet.

"What, uh, are you doing out here?" he asked stupidly.

"Came out for a quick cigarette."

"Shouldn't smoke you know, it's a disg—" Matt started to say out of habit and nervousness.

"—disgusting habit! Yeah, yeah! Don't lecture

me, Matt – I'm in too good a mood," Cat snapped. "Anyway, what are you doing out here on your own?"

"Catrina, about me and Tasha—" Matt began, wondering what he could say to explain how he was feeling. He hoped being straight with her might work. But it didn't.

"Give it a rest! I don't want to hear about you two again!"

"Come on, Cat! All that stuff's in the past now. And maybe you and me..."

"You and me what, Matt? Listen, for the sake of everyone else, I may forgive you, but I'll never forget what you did to me," she hissed.

"Cat... I—"

"Forget it, Matt. Anyone'd think you really cared. Not quite your style, is it?"

Catrina turned on her kitten heel and headed back inside.

Matt slumped back down on to the step and stared up at the stars. He'd blown it. Again.

• • •

Stomping towards Ollie, Elaine and Jakey, who were all dancing together to some silly old Kylie hit, Cat quickly wiped the tears from her eyes.

Somehow, she'd hoped that she and Matt

might get back together tonight, but she'd been caught out bumping into him like that and hadn't been able to hold her tongue.

She'd blown it, she knew. But no one else was going to.

Cat forced her features into a beaming grin.

"Got another hug for your Catwoman?" she asked, throwing her arms around Ollie.

"'Course," he grinned, giving her a great big bear-hug. "You saved the day, Cat. The whole thing could've been a disaster without you and your bright idea!"

Catrina twinkled at him. "Well, I like to think I'd help a friend in need, Ollie."

"Listen, are you OK?" asked Ollie, holding her round the waist and looking into her still glistening eyes."

"Yes!" she said as brightly as she could, but giving herself away by glancing over quickly at the café door.

Ollie spotted Matt's downcast expression as he sat on the step outside and stared back in at the party.

"Catrina..." said Ollie slowly, realisation dawning on him.

"Uh-huh?"

"Is this hug for Matt's benefit?"

Cat opened her mouth as if to say something

then closed it again and gave him a sweet smile instead.

"And let me guess..." Ollie continued, his eyes suddenly open to much of what had gone on over the past few weeks. "All that business with you and me. Was that all for Matt's benefit too?"

"Oh, Ollie!" simpered Catrina, opening her eyes as wide as she could. "You're not annoyed with me, are you?"

"I should be," replied Ollie with mock sternness, "but I'm too happy tonight to be angry."

"And I saved your show remember!" she grinned at him, before taking his hands from round her waist and placing them round Elaine's. "He's all yours!"

As Elaine laughed, Cat did a little twirl then shimmied her way around Jakey.

• • •

"Have you seen Joe or Matt?" Sonja asked Anna, who was standing behind the counter, surveying the heaving room in front of her and taking a well-earned breather from serving endless food and drinks to the revellers. True to form, Nick had wandered off and found some luckless female to chat up.

"No, sorry," said Anna, who had – despite being rushed off her feet – seen both Matt and Joe leave. But Anna recognised their need to be alone and didn't think it would do any good to go telling Sonja right now and spoil *her* fun.

Sonja leant back against the cool metal of the counter and scanned the room again for the two boys. But instead of Joe or Matt, she saw Kerry, who was staring off into the dance floor.

What's she looking so fed up about? wondered Sonja as she shuffled her way back to her friend. As she squeezed her way over, she had to laugh at the fact that no one seemed to have noticed that the cranky old jukebox was doing its favourite old trick when it began to overheat: slowing down and speeding up.

Well, that'll soon be the end of this party, she smiled to herself, knowing that the music was only about a record away from being so distorted that people wouldn't be able to stand it.

As soon as Sonja arrived by Kerry's side, she saw the problem: Mick was standing with his back to her, very obviously chatting up a flummoxed-looking Maya.

And that wasn't all. Following Kerry's gaze, she saw what was holding her attention – Ollie was still dancing, but was now also kissing Elaine. A long, lingering kiss.

"Just good friends then?" Sonja said wryly.

"Doesn't look like it," shrugged Kerry. "And it doesn't look like you're a great matchmaker either!"

Before Sonja had to admit she got it wrong about Mick, Cat – breathless from dancing – appeared in front of the two girls.

"So, what did you think? Wasn't I brilliant?"

Sonja grinned at her cousin. "Yep, you certainly were, Cat. We were very surprised and very impressed. Weren't we, Kerry?"

"Totally. Great costume, Cat. Did you make it?"

"I certainly did. Another of my many talents. Like making up great dance routines *and* riding motorbikes – eh, Jakey?" she cackled.

Cat reached over and stroked the shiny head of Elaine's mate as he beamed back at her like a lovesick puppy.

Sonja swapped a knowing glance with Kerry. Catrina had that predatory look in her eye again...

Which just goes to show, thought Sonja ruefully. *A leopard-print Catwoman never quite changes her spots.*

Sugar
SECRETS...

...& Rivals

SNEAK PREVIEW!

"And she thought I'd make a brilliant model, said I had the right figure and face and *everything*!" Sonja stood in front of the full-length mirror in her room and studied her figure with appreciation.

"Natasha was convinced I'd be snapped up straight away if I went for it," she continued. "Isn't that great?"

Kerry lowered the magnified mirror she had been using to peer critically at her face. "It's *sickeningly* great," she replied, a touch of bitterness in her voice. "What did God think he was doing when he dished out people's looks?"

Sonja spun round to face her friend, a mystified look on her face. She wasn't entirely sure what Kerry was going on about.

"I mean, look at you," Kerry went on. "There you are, tall, tanned and gorgeous. Perfect figure, looks to die for, nice teeth, shiny hair. You eat like a pig and stay stick thin. Then there's me..."

Kerry leapt up from the bed and stood in front of the mirror next to Sonja.

"Just look at it," she grumbled, stretching her arms out wide in despair. "Short, lumpy, fat thighs, huge arse, no boobs, hair I can't do a bloody thing with, blind as a bat. Complete stinking failure, actually!"

Sonja stared wide-eyed at her friend, astonished by the intensity of her unexpected outburst. Kerry was obviously having a Bad Hair Day, or suffering from PMT, or something.

"Don't be silly, Kez," she clucked, soothingly. "I don't know what you're complaining about – you're really attractive."

"Yeah, compared to a pig, perhaps!" Kerry took off her glasses and squinted into the mirror. A blurry blob with frizzy hair squinted back. "Mind you, not even pigs have got eyesight as bad as mine," she sighed dramatically.

"For God's sake, stop whingeing," Sonja chided. "I mean, it could be worse – you could look like Cat." She chuckled a little. "Now, as I was saying, Tasha was really encouraging. She said I had great bone structure, perfect for being a model. What do you think?"

"I think Natasha is absolutely right, you'd make a great model," Kerry said magnanimously. "If that's what you really want to do, then you should go for it."

"Well, that's the thing, isn't it? I don't, at least not in the long term."

"So *why* are you going on about it?" Kerry demanded a little irritably.

"I'm not! I just wanted your opinion, that's all. But if you're in such a foul mood I won't bother..."

Sonja gave Kerry a withering look which

immediately made her friend wish she'd kept her mouth shut. Of course Sonja was right – she *was* in a foul mood and had been since she'd got to Sonja's house two hours ago.

They often met up at each other's homes to get ready for a night out together (mostly at Sonja's because she had more space). They usually had a couple of drinks while they got changed, experimented with different clothes, listened to CDs and generally got into the party mood.

But tonight, ever since Kerry had arrived, all Sonja had done was go on and on about blasted Natasha and what a 'laugh' they'd had the previous evening. She hadn't even thought to ask how Kerry was, what sort of day she'd had or anything remotely to do with anyone else.

And when Kerry had tried to change the subject and ask if there was any news about Joe, Sonja admitted that she and Natasha had been having *such* a great time at the café, she'd completely forgotten to call on Ollie. They'd even gone to the pictures together and caught the later showing of the film she was supposed to have seen with Matt.

"Ooh, come on, hurry up," Sonja announced looking at her watch. "I told Tasha we'd meet her at eight. Mustn't be late."

No, we couldn't possibly be late for Tasha, Kerry thought bitterly. *It wouldn't do to keep poor Tasha waiting, would it? Never mind that I've spent hours of my life waiting for Sonja to turn up because she's hardly ever on time. Oh no, suddenly we must all break our backs just because it's ruddy Natasha!*

Kerry deliberately took her time finishing her nails; she had already decided that this was going to be a really bad night out.

Sonja grabbed her bag from the dresser, opened the door and waved at Kerry to follow her, which she dutifully did. The girls then made the short walk to the bar where they had arranged to meet Natasha.

As she walked through the door, Kerry half expected to see Matt or Catrina or one of the others. But tonight there were only the faces of people she barely knew. Oh, and Natasha sitting on a bar stool already being chatted up by a suave-looking older guy in a posh suit and tie.

Catching the girls' eyes as they walked in, Natasha pulled a 'help me' face over the guy's shoulder. Immediately taking the initiative, Sonja strode over to where they were sitting and touched Natasha's bare thigh.

"Sorry I'm late, darling," she cooed, "I got held up. I hope no one's been hassling you."

She leant over and kissed Natasha on the lips.

The guy at the bar's eyes nearly popped out of his head while Kerry hung back in the doorway, deeply embarrassed by Sonja's spot of acting.

"Uh, no," Natasha replied, immediately cottoning on. "This is John. John – meet my girlfriend."

Crimson-faced, the poor guy was already beginning to beat a hasty retreat. Once he was out of sight, the duo collapsed in hysterics and the tone of the evening was set.

As Kerry had expected, it was the start of a rotten night playing second fiddle to the Sonja and Natasha show. And even though she couldn't find any particular reason to hate Ollie's sister, the fact that she and Sonja seemed to have such a good time together was enough to make Kerry retreat into a shell of unease in their company. The fact that they didn't even seem to notice that Kerry was there didn't improve the situation.

Half-way through the evening Natasha suggested they go to a club called Henry's.

"I used to go there all the time when I lived at home," she beamed. "I know Henry and he used to let me in even though I was only fourteen. He thought I was much older, tarted up in make-up and heels and little dresses. It was such a hoot!

The music's great and there's always tasty guys there. C'mon, what do you say?"

Kerry didn't know what to say. Henry's had always looked a bit sleazy to her from the outside and she'd never had any desire to go in there at all.

"Oh wow, yeah, great! Let's go!" Sonja hollered before Kerry could think of a way to wriggle out of it.

Without bothering to find out what Kerry wanted to do, Natasha and Sonja left the bar and began heading up the street towards Henry's. Reluctantly, Kerry tagged along behind.

As soon as they got inside the club, Kerry's heart sank even further. The place had changed hands several times since Natasha had last been there and with dingy lighting, faded soft furnishings and floors that your feet stuck to as you walked, it looked as if it had seen better times.

Still, there was a dance floor and music – and that was all the girls needed really.

Sonja and Natasha immediately made a beeline for the dance floor and began grooving wildly to an obscure '70s track. In no mood to join them, Kerry found a seat on the edge of the dance floor, wishing she was at home with a cup of hot chocolate and a *Friends* video.

IS SHE REALLY YOUR BEST MATE?

• •

She's meant to be your best mate, but lately she's been more like an enemy. We've all been in Kerry's shoes at one time or another! Put your friendship to the test with our top quiz...

Nobody's perfect, but a *real* friend is someone who you should be able to trust, who should always be there for you and who you can feel totally relaxed with.

Read the following and decide whether each statement is **TRUE** or **FALSE** for you – then see if your best friend's actually doing her job!

I. **Does she make you feel happy?**

• "There are times when she makes me feel inadequate."
• "She often snaps at me."
• "I get the feeling I'm boring her."
• "She takes the mick out of me constantly."
• "She laughs at a lot of my opinions."
• "It's like she tries to outdo me all the time."

2 How loyal is she?

- "She's started to spend more time with her other mates, instead of me."
- "I sometimes think she's talking about me behind my back."
- "She's easily impressed with other people, and swayed by their opinions."
- "She sometimes puts me down in front of others."
- "She's let me down more than once lately."
- "She seems to have private jokes and conversations with other friends – and I'm not included."

3 Are the bonds between you still strong?

- "We don't seem to be as close as we once were."
- "She can be pretty secretive, as if she doesn't want me to share things."
- "I used to tell her everything, but don't feel like I can now."
- "I don't know what she's thinking any more."
- "We argue more than we used to."
- "We don't hang out as much as we used to."

4 Does she take advantage of you?

- "She expects me to drop everything when *she's* in the mood to hang out."
- "She's always too busy telling me about *her* life to listen to what's going on in mine."
- "She just expects me to go along with *her* plans all the time."
- "She sometimes comes out with hurtful comments without meaning to, as if she hasn't thought before she's opened her mouth."
- "She's always telling me how brilliant another friend is without ever saying anything nice about *me*."
- "I think my feelings come *way* down her list of priorities."

COUNT UP HOW MANY TIMES YOU ANSWERED **TRUE** AND HOW MANY TIMES YOU ANSWERED **FALSE** FOR EACH SECTION, THEN TURN THE PAGE TO SEE WHAT IT MEANS...

SO, IS SHE A GREAT MATE OR NOT?

• •

If you answered **TRUE** once or twice in each section

Don't panic – your friendship is still pretty solid.
So, you've got the odd little niggle, but it's
nothing the two of you can't sort out during a
girls'-night-in with giant bag of tortilla chips and
a good heart-to-heart chat.

And while your mate might have her faults,
are you entirely guilt-free? Or could you be
overreacting to the situation?

Is that what's happening with Kerry? Or is
she right to worry about what's going on with
her friendship?

If you answered **TRUE** three or more times in each section

Your friendship could be failing. If you've shared
good times in the past, then it's probably worth
trying to work your hassles out – so get her
round to your place and tell her straight how
she's been letting you down and getting you down.

But of course, being that up front with
someone is often easier said than done, as Kerry's
finding out...

Sugar
SECRETS...
...& Rivals

FRIENDS!
Kerry can count on Sonja 100% –
they've been best friends forever.

BETRAYAL!
Then Ollie's sister turns up and things
just aren't the same any more.

RIVALS!
How can Kerry possibly hope to
compete with the glamorous Natasha...?

*Some secrets are just too good to
keep to yourself!*

Collins
An Imprint of HarperCollinsPublishers
www.fireandwater.com

Sugar
SECRETS...
...& Lies

CONFESSIONS!
Is Ollie in love? Yes? No? Definitely
maybe!

THE TRUTH!
Sonja is determined to find out who the
lucky girl can be.

LIES!
But someone's not being honest, which
might just break Kerry's heart...

*Some secrets are just too good to
keep to yourself!*

Collins
An Imprint of HarperCollins*Publishers*
www.fireandwater.com

Sugar
SECRETS...
...& Freedom

FAMILIES!
They can drive you insane, and Maya's
at breaking point with hers.

GUILT!
There's tragedy in store – but is Joe
partly to blame?

FREEDOM!
The price is high, so who's going to
pay...?

*Some secrets are just too good to
keep to yourself!*

Collins
An Imprint of HarperCollinsPublishers
www.fireandwater.com

Sugar
SECRETS...

...& Lust

DATE-DEPRIVATION!
Sonja laments the lack of fanciable
blokes around, then two come along at
once.

MYSTERY STRANGER!
One is seriously cute, but why is he
looking for Anna?

LUST!
Will Sonja choose Kyle or Owen –
or both?!

*Some secrets are just too good to
keep to yourself!*

Collins
An Imprint of HarperCollinsPublishers
www.fireandwater.com

Order Form

To order direct from the publishers, just make a list of the titles you want and fill in the form below:

Name ....

Address ....

....

....

Send to: Dept 6, HarperCollins Publishers Ltd, Westerhill Road, Bishopbriggs, Glasgow G64 2QT.

Please enclose a cheque or postal order to the value of the cover price, plus:

UK & BFPO: Add £1.00 for the first book, and 25p per copy for each additional book ordered.

Overseas and Eire: Add £2.95 service charge. Books will be sent by surface mail but quotes for airmail despatch will be given on request.

A 24-hour telephone ordering service is available to Visa and Access card holders: 0141- 772 2281

Collins
An *Imprint* of HarperCollins*Publishers*